I0563654

Copyright ©2015 by Pattie Doss. Publisher: Exquisite Reads Publications, LLC.

All rights reserved. No part of this book may be reproduced, stored in a retrieval system or transmitted by any means, electronic, mechanical, photocopying, recording, or otherwise, without the express written permission of publisher, except by a reviewer who may quote brief passages to be printed online, in a newspaper or magazine.

This is a work of FICTION. Names, characters, places, and incidents are products of the author's imagination or are used fictitiously and are not to be assumed as real. Any resemblance to actual events, locales, organizations, or persons, living or dead, is entirely coincidental.

ACKNOWLEDGMENTS

I give all praises to God for this incredible talent and the ability to be able to do something that I love. To see so many of my dreams coming true is truly a blessing and one that I don't take for granted.

I would like to thank my readers and fans of my **SOMEBODY ELSE'S HUSBAND SERIES.** I never dreamed this series would have become as well-known as it has. I couldn't have done it without you guys. Thanks for taking a chance on me and supporting a new author.

To my best friend Oreal Clemons, thank you for supporting me on this journey. You have been with me from the idea of book one to this book and I could never, ever repay you for everything you've done for me. Thanks for taking on different roles and responsibilities to help me with my business and my books. Most of all thanks for being a good friend.

To my Shenna, as always thanks for being there through another book. I know I probably drove you crazy with the test reads, questions, characters, plots, etc. Just know that I appreciate, everything you have done for me.

To my family, thanks for your continued support of my writing. Special thanks to my big sister, Ann from New York that pushes my books throughout the East Coast! I truly appreciate all that you have done for me. For my brother, Gerone, thank you for pushing my books in Mississippi.

Big thanks to my sisters and brothers in the literary world, as well that has been so supportive to me and my endeavors. A special shout-out goes to Angel Walker for the beautiful cover, Xyla Turner, Phylicia Allen, Shatisha Nash, Jessica Wren, Thalia Lake, Venessia Randle, Dorian Wilson, Bianca Harrison, Niyah Moore, Frederick Brooks, Ambitious Williams, Lauryn Lashley, Gina Lewis, Kelvin Brown, Shannika Pippins, Holli Jenkins, Conquella DS, Ebony Evans, and other readers and authors that may have shared a link or post or recommended my book, THANK YOU!

A VERY SPECIAL SHOUT OUT TO SOUTHERN GIRLS BOOK CLUB (SGBC) OF JACKSON, MS FOR INDUCTING ME AS AN HONORARY MEMBER OF THEIR BOOK CLUB.

Last but not least a very big thank-you goes out to my husband, Detric and my children: Dakiriyah, Detric II, and DaNiyah who allow me time away from being a mother and wife to write! I love you guys!

Authoress Patti Doss

Last time on Somebody Else's Husband, Too

PERSIA

It has been days since the incident at the house with Derek. Things were a mess that day. The kids came home and saw the police leaving. So, I had to sit them down and talk to them. It was the hardest thing I ever had to do but I had to do it. But the kids seemed to be taking it okay. However, Aaliyah asked if she could at least call her daddy because she missed him. I told her that I would call him later for her to talk to him. Derek Jr. just looked at me. I knew he had questions, and I knew he was angry, but he didn't want his little sister to see him that way, so he said okay and hurriedly went to his room. Times like this, I needed Tammie around, but she was on her way to Hawaii. Looking at my daughter, I saw the pain in her eyes. As a mother, it pained me to see her hurt, so I decided to try to ease the hurt she was feeling.

I dialed Derek's number and gave the phone to Aaliyah while I went upstairs behind DJ to see if he was okay.

When I reached the room, I found him on the bed crying. He wasn't moaning, or hollering but the tears were flowing from his eyes. I wanted to say something to comfort him, but I knew no words would help, so I just grabbed him and hugged him tight. As I hugged him, he began to cry louder and louder. With every tear, my heart broke just a little bit more. Aside from working, Derek had never been out of the kids' lives and it was weighing heavily on DJ that his mother and father were not going to be together anymore. Before I could say anything to him, I heard Aaliyah coming up the stairs.

"Mommy, the phone is for you," she said. I laid DJ back down on his bed and got up to answer the phone.

"Persia, I don't want to argue with you. I'm sorry for everything I've done. I just want to spend some time with my children. Please just let me see them," Derek said, begging into the phone. I could hear the hurt and pain in his voice, and I know he was sincerely missing the kids. I looked at DJ curled up in the fetal position on his bed and at that moment, nothing mattered but making my babies happy again.

"I'm sorry for what I did too. I shouldn't have disrespected you like that, but I will never keep the kids from you. You are welcome to see them," I said as the tears started to well up in my eyes.

"Thank you so much! Now please come open the door for me," he said. I moved the phone from my ear and headed down the stairs to the front door and opened it. On the other side was Derek, with tons of bags for the kids at his feet and a teddy bear holding a heart that said, *I'm sorry!* Derek handed me the teddy bear and when I grabbed the bear, he pulled me to him and kissed me. I quickly broke the kiss and stepped back, as he grabbed the bags and came on into the house. I put my finger up to my lips, signaling for him to be quiet as we both tiptoed up the steps. I stopped him at the top of the stairs as I went ahead into DJ's room. When I got in the room, Aaliyah was sitting on the bed near her brother trying to console him with tears rolling down her face.

"Kids, I have a surprise for you."

DJ slowly sat up and wiped his face and Aaliyah did the same. I left out of the doorway and told Derek to go ahead. I stood back as Derek entered DJ's room. From the sounds coming from that room, you would have thought my kids were meeting President Obama.

Tears flowed from my eyes as I realized that no matter what Derek did to me, he will always be a part of my life. If Tammie and Mike could come back from the bad patch in their marriage, who's to say that Derek and I couldn't work things out in our relationship?

The one time I wanted Tammie to psychoanalyze me, her ass was on a plane headed to paradise. Even though Tammie was not there physically, I'd been around her long enough to know what she would say. *If you think there is something still there, there is nothing wrong with fighting for what you believe in.* She may not say it that exact way but I was almost certain it would be something like that.

Hearing the happiness and joy in that room, I knew three things. One; I could never take Derek out of my kids life. Two; despite everything that happened between us, I still loved that man with everything in me. Three; I wanted my family back.

So, I wiped my face, held my head up and joined my family in DJ's room. Derek and I stayed in there with the kids until they fell asleep. They were so overwhelmed at having their dad home again that they went to sleep quickly.

Derek and I went downstairs to talk. As we sat on the couch, Derek pulled an envelope out of his pocket and handed it to me. Inside of it was two folded letters. The first one I pulled out was a *Complaint for Divorce*. My heart stopped beating and I looked up at Derek as he said, "Read it." I thought Derek was serving me with divorce papers, but the papers were for him and Keisha. He had filed for divorce from Keisha.

"Her papers will be served to her by the Constable in a couple of days. Persia, I'm sorry for everything I did to you. I hurt you so bad. I don't care about the past. I just want a fresh start and a chance to make everything right again. Read the second letter. It says the things I want to say that I couldn't."

I opened the letter and it started, "*Dear Persia, I'm not good at writing down my thoughts and feelings, but I guess this time I have to make an exception. First off, I just want you to know that I love you. I always did and I always will. Before all this happened, I thought I couldn't decide. I didn't know who I wanted to be with so I was selfish and tried to hold on to you both, but the truth is I did know. I was just too greedy to follow my heart. Maybe it was out of fear or maybe it was just pure stupidity. Whatever it was, I regret it. It took me losing you to realize what you mean to me. I don't know why men insist on learning things the hard way. Maybe we are wired that way. All I know is that since I lost you, nothing seems right anymore. I miss you and I miss our kids. I'm not going to ask you to take me back or give me another chance because I don't deserve one. I hurt you so bad and so deeply. All I ask is that you forgive me. Please don't let what I did to you turn you into someone you are not. Don't let me be the reason you stop believing in love. I want you to love again, even if it's not with me. I love you, Persia. I'm so sorry for ever putting my hands on you. If nothing else, I hope that for the sake of our children, we learn to be friends again. I love you, Persia, and always will, Derek!"*

After reading the letter, I didn't know what to say to Derek, because the truth was I still loved him just as much as he loved me, but at this point, was love enough?

"I love you, Derek. How could I not? You're the father of my children and the man I thought was my husband for years. Love is not a fountain or a light switch; I can't just turn it on and off. The love I have for you may have changed a little bit, but it hasn't disappeared. I don't know what the future holds for us, but for now I do forgive you."

"Sometimes two people have to fall apart before they realize that they truly belong together. I wanted a perfect ending. What girl doesn't? Now I've learned the hard way that there is no perfect ending or happily ever after. Life is about not knowing, having to change and adjust, and taking the moments and making the best out of it, without knowing what's going to happen next. That's why we have faith, hope, and, most of all, love. Right now, love is all we have and the only way that we can help each other."

EXQUISITE READS PUBLICATIONS

SOMEBODY ELSE'S HUSBAND, AGAIN:

RACHEL'S STORY

PATTI DOSS

PROLOGUE

All my life, I've let men use me. I've had this crazy urge to want unattainable men and let them walk all over me, just so I could feel like somebody loved me. Many people say the rape has a lot to do with my relationships with men. I'll admit that it did play a part in it, but my problems started long before I was raped. Dealing with an alcoholic mom who loved to party didn't make my life any easier either. From the constant moving because Mom wouldn't pay the bills to living in a house with the lights or water off because my momma gambled or drunk up the money; those events played a part as well.

Where was my father, you may ask?

I was a side baby. My mom was a side chick to a married man. She got pregnant and he got ghost. I only met my father three times that I can remember. I met him once when I was about five or six then again when I was nine and each time, he barely paid me any attention. He only talked to me because he was trying to get with my mom. I don't even think he wanted to be a family with us. He just wanted my mom to continue to be his side chick, somebody he could fuck whenever he was horny and his wife wasn't putting out. The last time I saw him when I was ten, at his funeral. He was driving drunk and hit a tree. When I found out, I didn't even cry. My momma cried like she lost the love of her life. I never understood how she loved him, even when he didn't do anything to support me.

Anyway, I put all that behind and tried to make the most of everything and move on with my life. When I started high school, I was determined to do just that. I was ready for a fresh start. I remember the first day of high school, I saw this fine ass, dark-skinned muscular guy with mysterious eyes. I was determined to make him mines. I even showed the guy to Tammie and Persia. Guess I moved too slowly because by the end of the week, Tammie and the guy, who I later found out was Michael Dawson, were dating! Once again, I moved past it, although deep down, I never forgot how Tammie betrayed me.

We grew up and had kids. Everyone got married except me. I was always the side chick not the main chick. What hurt the most was the fact that Tammie and Michael got married. I kept thinking that if I had gotten the opportunity to talk to him, then maybe he would have married me and I would have had the perfect life. So when I saw a chance to fuck up her happiness, I did. I knew Mike was a cheater all along. He secretly cheated on Tammie with several cheerleaders. I never told Tammie because honestly, I was glad he was fucking around on her. I don't know why I didn't just go sleep with Mike when we were in high school. I guess I really did value my friendship with Tammie. As we got older, she got this chip on her shoulder like she was so perfect and the rest of us were just fuck ups, well me anyways. She always had a smart remark or advice on what I needed to do in my life. So, when she started talking to Persia about her suspicions of Mike cheating on her, I knew I could seduce him.

The day I seduced Mike, I knew Tammie wasn't home. So I put on a sexy outfit, made up an excuse to go to her house, and decided to let nature take its course. I knew Tammie wasn't big on giving head, so I knew Mike wouldn't turn down any head. He was a little hesitate at first, but he quickly relaxed and enjoyed himself. All it took was that one time, and he was hooked—literally. We fucked like rabbits until my damn feelings got involved and then I wanted him all to myself. Of course he wasn't going for that, but after I ended up pregnant, I thought I had a chance to be with him. I was wrong and my pregnancy gave him an epiphany to do right by Tammie, but he stepped up and handled his responsible to my boys, Mikele and Mikye.

Even though I fell in love with Mike, I'm starting to face the fact that he doesn't want me. I was just the side chick. STORY OF MY LIFE....

1

PERSIA

Watching Derek and the kids sleep, I couldn't help but wonder if I was doing the right thing by giving this relationship another try.

Can our relationship really be saved? Are we just holding on because we are afraid to let go? These are the questions that are constantly running through my mind.

Rubbing my hands over Derek's wavy hair and smooth, chocolate skin, I couldn't help but think about my family. I love Derek and I'll always love him. The kids are ecstatic to have him home again, but again I ask myself, *is that enough?*

The fact that I have a lot of questions with very few answers tells me that we still have some things to work out. Part of me

Am I basing my decision on my love for Derek or because of the kids? So many questions were plaguing my mind.

Just as my mind start to go overboard with the *what-if* situations, the doorbell rang. The clock on my nightstand read 11:08

p.m. I eased out of bed with Derek and the kids and went to answer the door.

"Who is it?" I asked. No one answered but I continue to hear movement outside the door.

"Who is it?" I ask a little louder than before.

There was silence for a few seconds then I heard a female voice say, "I'm looking for Derek!"

Feelings of de ja vu covered my entire body. I couldn't open the door fast enough but my eyes weren't prepared for what they were seeing.

On the other side of the door was the most gorgeous person, I've ever seen. I wasn't sure if it was a woman or man at first until I spotted his Adam's apple and looked at his feet to see shoes that looked like a size 12 or 13. It was definitely a guy, but he was prettier than any woman, I'd seen in a long time.

He was light-skinned with hazel eyes and long brown tresses flowing down his back with light gold highlights in the front. He had on ripped jeans with a fitted V-neck shirt and red canvas sneakers. His makeup was done perfectly, not a lash was out of place. I was so fixated on his beauty that I almost forgot that he was looking for Derek.

Before I could say something, he spoke. "Is Derek here? He asked nervously.

"Yes, he is. Who's asking?" I asked as calmly as I could.

"No offense, but I'd rather not discuss that with you. Can I please talk to Derek?" the beautiful man said in a pleading manner.

I give him credit for not being the messy type, it seemed he really was trying to address the situation in a passive manner.

"Well, I'm the wife and seeing how I don't know you, I would like to know what you want with my husband?"

"No offense, but you're not the wife. Derek's wife is named Keisha. Can you please just let Derek know that I'm here?" the man said sternly.

All I saw was RED. I counted to ten in my head to try to come down before I did something I would regret. I refused to let another one of Derek's shenanigans get me out of character again. I was wrong about him not being the messy type. He was definitely trying to start some shit by even showing up on my doorstep.

"Ok, wait here. I'll get Derek for you! What is your name?" I said through clenched teeth.

The man replied, "I'm Taylor, he knows me."

It was taking everything in me not to snap. Determined not to snoop down to his level, I quickly counted to ten in my head and said a couple of whoo-sas.

I closed the door on Taylor and went upstairs. I woke Derek up and signaled for him to follow me downstairs. I stopped at the last step and pointed to the door, "Somebody wants to see you."

"Who is it?" Derek asked sleepily.

"Open the door and see!" I replied.

I stood off to the side, so I could see the look on his face once he sees Taylor's.

Derek opens the door and his eyes gets as big as an owl. He stepped onto the stoop where Taylor was and tried to say something but no words would come out. He looked back at me and I smiled at him. There was no point in yelling at him or causing a scene. I needed to make a decision about us, and that decision just got easier to make.

With a bigger smirk on his face from seeing Derek in shock, Taylor spoke up. "Can I talk to you alone, please?"

Derek looked at me with guilt all over his face and tears filled his eyes.

"Go ahead. I've seen all I need to see. Good night, Taylor! Can't say it was nice to meet you, but I do love your hair!

I closed my door and locked it. Sometimes what you're most afraid of doing is the very thing that will set you free. I was afraid to let go, but this gave me the push I need to realize that sometimes the hardest thing to do is the best thing to do.

After a few minutes, I heard banging on the door.

"Open the door, Persia! Persia, I know you hear me!" Derek was screaming at the door. I guess he got rid of his secret lover, Taylor.

I grabbed his phone, keys, and his shoes and put them on the back porch and walked back to the front door.

"Your keys and shoes are on the back porch. Take them and get the fuck away from me. Don't call, text, or come by. When I am ready to talk to you, I may call you but just so we clear, 'DEREK, IT'S OVER!' You come back apologizing like you really want you family back, but I guess Taylor just slipped your mind, huh? Don't answer that, I'm already sick to my stomach. Just get away from here now before I call the police and this time I will press charges," I yelled through the door at Derek.

He started to say something, but he stopped. I heard him get his keys and stuff off the back porch. After a while, I heard him pull out the driveway.

I couldn't go back to sleep so I made me some coffee and watched old movies on Netflix.

2

DEREK

It's true what they say, *what's done in the dark comes to the light!* Never in a million years would I have thought that Taylor would come to Persia's house. I ended things with her as soon as Persia found out about Keisha.

Taylor was born Tyler. Yes, Taylor was born a man, but believe me, she is all woman now. To some people it may seem weird that I'm cool with that, but I don't care what others think. No, I'm not gay. Taylor is a woman, mind, body, soul, and legally. That's how I see her and that's how I'll always see her.

Taylor was cool. I met her in Nashville and she immediately captured my attention. She was gorgeous with the prettiest smile, I've ever seen. Even though she was in khakis and her red *Family Dollar* shirt, her curvaceous figure was still visible. She was working the load I delivered to the store.

We ended up conversing and I learned that she attended Tennessee State University, studying Business. Since I was going to be in Tennessee for a few days, I asked her about some of the local night spots. She told me about a few spots and invited me to a party later that day.

Taylor was so easy to talk to that I ended up telling her about Keisha and Persia. She even tried to convince me to tell them before they found out on their own.

She wasn't like most girls that wanted to be with a truck driver for the thrill. Taylor was actually intrigued by the fact that I got to drive all over the country and she seemed genuinely interested in me or so I thought.

Towards the end of the night, I asked her to dance, since we had talked for most of the party. She agreed and we danced to *Baby Hold On TO Me* by Gerald Levert. As we danced, she sang along. She actually had a beautiful voice. At the end of the song, I went in for a kiss but she stopped me and went back and sat down.

I was confused and my ego was hurt a little. I followed her back the table where we were sitting and sat down.

"I have to tell you something Derek," Taylor said fidgeting with her fingers in her lap.

"What is it? I asked as I lifted her head up so I could look in her face.

"My name wasn't always Taylor. My birth name was Tyler," she said and lowered her head again.

"It took a few seconds before my mind processed what she said, but when it did. I hopped up and prepared to leave."

"Derek, wait let me explain, please," Taylor said. "I was born a man, but I now I am all woman.

"Regardless, you are still a man and I'm not gay, Taylor."

"Derek, from everything you have already told me, I know that you are not gay. I don't consider myself gay either. I am as much of a woman as any other woman, I just wasn't born one! I'm not looking for a man, and honestly honey you already got your plate full, if I was interested in you, which I'm not. So, how about you keep your assumptions to yourself and let's enjoy the rest of the night."

"Taylor, I'm sorry. I jumped to conclusions. Thank you for telling me that. Now that we got that out the way, I don't see why we can't be friends."

We talked about everything from books to the POTUS. Taylor was a very interesting person and she was very intelligent.

As we talked, my mind still couldn't register that Taylor was really a man, because deep down inside I was semi-attracted to her.

I have never been attracted to a man! Never had the urge to rub, feel, touch, or fuck a man, but Taylor had me discombobulated like a motherfucker.

"Can I ask you a personal question, Taylor?"

"I think I know what you want to ask, but go ahead."

"Did you have a sex change?"

"Yes, Derek. I had the sex change operation," She stated with a short giggle. She had been asked that question so much that she has learned to expect it.

"Wow! I mean that like intriguing. I always wondered how they do that."

"Well, if you that interested in it, I could just show you and you tell me if they did a good job or not?" Taylor suggested.

"Nah, that's not necessary. I'll take your word for it."

"Come on, you know you want to. I promise I won't tell anyone. Also, you're not even from here, so who would I tell?" She explained.

"You got a point, but nah let's just keep things like we have them."

"Okay, you had your chance, you may not get another one."

"Okay, I am curious. I want to see it!"

Taylor got up and grabbed my hand, pulling me up out of my chair. I followed her to the area by the bathrooms. Once the coast was clear, she pulled me into the men's bathroom and locked the door.

"Sit on the toilet! Close your eyes! No peeking!" She demanded.

After about a minute, I felt Taylor in front of me. I opened my eyes and she was completely NAKED and like she said, she was .all woman.

She had perfectly round breasts that looked to be about a 38 or 40C, beautiful soft skin with a purple butterfly beneath her navel.

When I looked down, I was expecting to see something that would tell me that she used to be a man, but I was shocked.

It looked just like a regular woman's vagina. I couldn't even say anything.

"Do you want to touch it?"

Before I could answer, she had walked over to me, took my hand and guided it to her opening.

Not only did it look like a woman's vagina, it felt like one. I've touched and pounded enough pussy to know.

As if it was trained, my fingers made their way inside Taylor's openings. I quickly pull my hand away and prepared to leave, but she stopped me and kissed me.

I tried to resist the feeling. I was saying no, but my body was telling me yes. Taylor kissed me harder and deeper until I kissed her back.

It was no turning back now, as Taylor kissed the side of my face, behind my ears and under my shirt. I stopped her long enough to take off my clothes.

I sat down on the toilet and got ready to pull Taylor to me, so she could ride me, but she dropped to her knees and took me in her mouth. She was as skilled in fellatio as she was with walking in stilettos.

Just as I was about to cum and tried to pull out, she wrapped her arms around my waist and pulled me back into her until my dick hit the back of her throat. I rubbed her hair and grabbed the back of her head until I released every drop down her throat and even then she continued sucking.

Once my dick was stiff hard again, pulled out of her mouth and prepared to fuck her from the back.

"Bend that ass over!"

I spread my t-shirt on the floor as a blanket. I reached in my pants and took out a condom and put it on.

I was kind nervous about fucking Taylor. Would I damage something? Would I tear something loose? All kinds of thoughts were going to my head.

She noticed my hesitation. "It's ok, baby! You won't hurt me; I'm a big girl!"

From the first time, I stuck my dick into Taylor, I was convinced that she was a woman. She felt just like a woman, if not better.

As I fucked Taylor, I grabbed a fistful of her long tresses and long-stroked the shit out of her. I thought she wouldn't be able to handle me but again, I was wrong. She matched my rhythm and for about thirty minutes, we played a game of tug-of-war until I finally won the game. During the last few minutes, I sped up until she tapped out. She put up quite the fight and the pussy was awesome! Now I see why so many players and actors were getting caught up with trannies, because the sex is awesome. Taylor had me hooked, I can't lie.

After that night, if I was in Tennessee at all, we were hooking up. If Persia never found out about Keisha then Taylor and I would have probably still been fuck buddies.

Taylor knows how I feel about Persia and my kids, so I cannot believe she just pulled a POP-UP on me. Any chances I had left were lost when Persia opened that door.

Since Taylor drove all this way to fuck up things between me and Persia, it's only fair that I fuck her up. I'm not taking about beating her up. I'm talking about beating that pussy down. Shit, why not at this point, I have nothing to fucking lose!

I picked up my phone and called Taylor. She finally answered on the fifth ring.

"Why did you do that? Why? Of all people, Taylor, I never expected you to be the messy type. It's not that I lied to you. I have told you the truth from the first day we met, so you already knew the deal. You knew what I wanted and who I wanted to be with. What were you thinking?

"Derek, I'm sorry. I wasn't thinking I just missed you so much and I couldn't call you because you blocked my number and I really needed to see you and talk to you, baby!

"Where are you now?"

"I'm staying at the *Holiday Inn Express* on Franklin Road, Room 36."

"Ok, I'll be there in a few. See you soon, we can talk then."

3

BRIAN

Another late night at the station. Normally, I hate when I'm working late, but tonight I was in no rush to go home. The peace and quiet will give me some time to think about things.

"Working late again, Brian?" Chico asked me interrupting my thoughts.

"Yeah, Nicole is gone out of town on a work trip, so no need to rush home to an empty house," I said.

"Well, since you got some free time, let's go to Stilettos, you need to relax a little. You been so uptight lately. What's been up with you? Chico asked me with concern in his voice.

"Nothing man. I'm alright. Thanks for asking though," I said.

"You sure? Nothing cheers me up better than seeing ass and breasts except maybe getting some new pussy, you know what I mean!" Chico said with a quick laugh as he rubbed his shiny bald head.

Not many people can pull off that look, but Chico had that "Common" look going on with the bald head and full beard. Women went crazy over it, especially since he was light-skinned with hazel eyes and the fact that he practically lived in the gym, took his "Common" effect, one step further.

"Come on, Brian. It's not even midnight yet. It's not like you got anything to do. I know Kandi can put a smile on your face because she definitely can put one on mines!" Chico said pleadingly.

From the many conversations I had with Chico about his strip club adventures and the way he would almost stalk Kandi when we went to Stilettos, I could tell Kandi was his favorite stripper.

Because Chico is at the club so regularly, he gathered so much information about Kandi and shared it with me. Kandi was not your typical stripper. She had the Three-B's that would make any man want to wife her up----beauty, brains, and booty. Kandi was a stripper but in the daytime, she went to Clark Atlanta University working on her Social Work degree.

Kandi was a twenty years old, Mississippi girl, that looked like Heather Hedley. She had a Coca-Cola bottle shape with one of those Mississippi Donks.

In case you don't know what a DONK is, it's bigger than a butt yet thicker and wider than an ass. Kandi had an ass that most Georgia girls paid for. People say everything is big in Texas, but they must never stopped in Mississippi because Mississippi girls have some of the fattest asses I've seen and it's not pumped with silicon or fix-a-flat.

"Nah man, I'm take a raincheck. I'm finish up here and head to the gym before going home," I said.

Chico responded, "Well tomorrow's my off day, so I'm about to make it rain all night. If you change your mind. Hit me up."

"Ok, man See you later," I said as we gave each other dab and went our separate ways. Truth was I could use a night out at Stilettos. I can't even remember the last time Nicole and I had sex. Everything been so stressful at home lately that sometimes, I purposely work late just to avoid arguing with her.

I tried to focus back on the report I was currently working on, but Chico's talk about ass and titties made me miss my wife Nicole. Things haven't been good between us lately. With the shortage of men on the force, I was required to work longer hours and more days, which barely left enough time for my wife. She worked in the daytime and I worked nights, so we rarely even see each other and when we do, all we do is argue.

We were becoming the old married couple we always said we wouldn't become, which is crazy because we don't have any children. You would think we have a fun, spontaneous relationship and sex life but we don't.

Nicole loves her job and I would never tell her to quit, but lately I've just been ready to start a family and Nicole doesn't want to. We've been into it on and off about it for a few days. So even though I'm thankful for the break from arguing, I do miss my wife a lot. I requested the days off work to go to Hawaii with her, but it was a last minute trip and since it wasn't a family emergency, my request was denied, especially since we are understaffed already.

Since Atlanta is six hours ahead of Hawaii, meaning it was only four in the evening in Hawaii. I called Nicole again to see how her trip was going. Her phone kept going to voicemail. Either she was still in a meeting or her phone wasn't picking up. I headed home but then I remember I had to stop by Wal-Mart.

I gathered my things, changed into my regular clothes, and left. Arriving at Wal-Mart, I was happy that it was not too crowded. I just had to pick up a few items and I would be out of there as quickly as I arrived. When I turned onto the coffee aisle, I almost ran right into a lady that was bent over tying her shoe. Her ass looked perfect in her black yoga pants and when she turned around, her face was almost as pretty as her ass looked. I know that a crazy comparison, but little momma had it going on.

She was a petite little thing, no more than 5'3, with a small bulge that looked like she was pregnant or just had a baby. Her light caramel skin tone matched the honey blonde streaks in her hair almost perfectly. She had a small, perfect circular mole above her lips. Her face was spotless except for that one little mole, but it didn't take anything from her beauty. She was gorgeous and although she was grown, she could pass for a teenager.

Snapping out of my thoughts, I finally found my voice, "Excuse me, I'm so sorry. I didn't see you, my mind was someplace else. I'm Brian and you are--?" I flashed her my most flirtatious smile. I don't know why I was flirting, but she was beautiful and I wanted to know her name.

"Hello, Brian. I'm Rachel. Goodbye Brian." She said, while returning her attention to deciding what kind of coffee she wanted. I tried to hide my disappointment at her answer, so she wouldn't know she bruised my ego a little.

"You are too beautiful to be so mean," I said to her flirting a little bit more and showing her my dimples. Women go crazy for my dimples and I knew she wouldn't be able to resist them either. I still had no idea why I was flirting. I never flirt with other women. Sure I'd steal a glance or something but normally I'd never do this.

"Look Brian. Your dimples are cute and your smile is infectious, but I have five kids waiting back at home for me. So before you give me your best line are you still interested? How about I answer it for you.....GOODBYE BRIAN!" She said before grabbing a bag of Dunkin Donuts Colombian Coffee.

I watched her walk away until she turned the corner. I could have tried harder, but I had no business flirting anyway. So I brushed it off and got my coffee and cream and preceded to pick up a few more items in the grocery section before heading to the bath and beauty aisle.

As soon as I hit the aisle with bath products, I saw Rachel.

"Are you following me?" She said with an attitude.

"No, Rachel! I'm not following you. I'm not a stalker, I'm a police officer and I just happen to need some soap!" I grabbed some soap and walked off, but she called my name.

"Brian! I'm sorry. I didn't mean to offend you," she said sincerely.

"It's ok. Enjoy the rest of your night," I said while walking off to the register to pay for my things.

Walking to my car, my mind was no longer on going home. I called Chico and told him I was on my way to the strip club.

"Hey man, you still at the club? I asked anxiously.

Yea man, I just got here. Are you coming? He asked me excitedly.

"Cool, ok! I'm here come on before I start the party without you," Chico said while laughing into the phone.

"Okay man, I'll see you in a few!" I said.

"Brian! Brian!"

I heard someone calling my name and turned to see who it was. It was Rachel. I walked towards her to see what she wanted.

"Just wanted to apologize one more time and to give you this," she said as she shoved a piece of paper into my hands and walked back into the store.

As I headed back to my car, I opened the folded paper and saw it was her phone number. I started to throw the number away, but I put the paper inside my wallet and smiled as pictures of Rachel's perfectly round ass danced in my head. I left Wal-Mart and headed to *Stilettos* to meet Chico.

***

Arriving at the club, I called Nicole again, but she still wasn't answering. I threw my phone in the glove compartment and went inside to meet Chico.

As expected, Chico was getting a lap dance from a stripper. It wasn't his favorite stripper, but this one was equally fine and thick. Her back was to me as she danced on Chico. She was light-skinned with long gold tresses flowing down her back. She had on a pink G-string that showed a big ass butterfly tattoo on her ass where the wings of the butterfly fell onto the cheeks of her ass. As she twerked and grinded on Chico's lap, the butterfly seemed to take flight. The more she twerked on Chico, the more the wings of the butterfly flapped. I waited until the song stopped and the stripper walked off before joining Chico at his table.

"I see you already got the party started. I need to catch up," I said while sitting down and noticing the empty shot glasses on the table.

"Yea, bruh. You got to catch up. You know I couldn't be around all this ass without some type of action," Chico responded.

Chico ordered more Patron shots and we watched the strippers do their thang. We even got lap dances from Sugar and Spice, the ghetto twin strippers. They were cute and had a nice body on them, but their bodies were covered in tattoos and they sound as if Ebonics was their first language. If you looked up ratchet in the dictionary, I'm almost certain you'd see their pictures.

Finally, Kandi was taking the stage and that was the moment that Chico was waiting on. He pulled out a wad of cash he had in a separate pocket and made his way closer to the stage. I followed him to the stage to get a closer look at his stripper crush.

Kandi danced to *It's like Candy* by *Cameo*. Watching her dance and seeing how all the men flocked to the stage when she danced, I could see why Chico was crazy about her. She danced with this nonchalant look on her face as her body moved gracefully and seductively on the stage.

She spotted Chico out of the crowd and moved to the side of the stage where he and I were. She gave Chico about 15 seconds of attention before maneuvering around the stage. I can't lie her dance was so seductive that it turned me on. I was hypnotized by her movements and her body.

At the end of Kandi's dance, she got a standing ovation and the stage was covered in money.

"Okay, now I understand why you stuck on Kandi," I said as we walked back to our table.

"I told you she was bad, man." Chico said still smiling from ear to ear.

"She is good. I'll admit that, but bruh you got it bad!" I said while make a whipping gesture with my hands.

After about thirty minutes or so, Kandi emerged from the back and started giving lap dances. I knew Chico was waiting for one. Kandi came over and gave him a lap dance. Surprisingly,

Kandi gave me a dance too. She danced from Chico's lap to mines. I'm sure Chico wasn't too happy about that.

Watching Kandi bounce, twerk, and shake her ass all over me and Chico, I couldn't help but think of our younger days and the many trains we pulled on girls like Kandi. After the dance, Chico signaled that he would be back. I knew he was going in the back room with Kandi so I just told him I'll see him tomorrow, It was almost four o'clock in the morning anyway.

Once I got to the car, I retrieved my phone to see if Nicole had called. She hadn't called me back nor texted me. I know she is on a business trip with the law firm she works with, but I know she wasn't too busy to send a text, leave a voicemail or something.

***

I arrived home and quickly showered and laid across the bed with the towel still wrapped around me. The house was so quiet, a little too quiet. I called Nicole again, but still didn't get any answer.

Picking my pants up off the floor to clean out my pockets before putting them in the hamper, Rachel's number fell out onto the floor. As much as I wanted to call her, I have never cheated on

Nicole and I didn't want to start now. So after cleaning up a bit, I went to bed.

Reaching out for Nicole, I woke up when I realized that she was not there. It took me a minute to realize that she was still on her trip and that I was alone. I looked at the clock and it was only a little after seven so it was too late to call Nicole.

I made a protein shake with the last of the almond milk before deciding to hit the gym.

Since it was early, the gym was basically empty. I worked out from around eight to ten. By the time I finished exercising, I was starving.

***

On the way home, I had to make a quick stop at Wal-Mart and pick up so milk while I was already out. Turning onto the milk aisle, who do I almost run into again.....Rachel.

"Okay, Mr. Officer I'm starting to think this is more than a coincidence," Rachel said to me sarcastically.

"Well you know what they say, *we don't meet people by coincidence, they are meant to cross our paths for a reason* so you just got to figure out what that reason is," I said cockily while flashing her a big smile.

"Well Ian Fleming would disagree. He would say, *Once is happenstance. Twice is coincidence. Three times is enemy action.* So Officer Brian, I hope I don't run into you a third time," she said sarcastically and walked away, headed to the baby formula section.

I paid for my milk and went into Subway and ordered me something to eat. As I was preparing to sit down and eat, I saw Rachel leaving. We must have saw each other at the same time because I waved goodbye to her and she just rolled her eyes. I flashed her a big smile and sat down to eat.

Rachel was a real cutie but she was not worth the trouble and something inside of me was telling me to *run! Run! Run!*

4

TAMMIE

After a long flight, we spent most of the day napping the jetlag away.

Around five p.m. I awoke to candles and rose petals everywhere. Mike was nowhere to be found. I followed the rose petals out to the beach and Mike was standing inside of a big heart drawn in the sand. When he saw me, he took a black ring box out of his pocket and dropped down on one knee.

By the time I reached him tears were falling from my eyes so bad, I could barely see. I wasn't sure if the tears fell because I was happy or because I simply did not know what to do. For years, I wanted Mike to show his appreciation for me and our love but he never did. His expressions of love was always done to ease his guiltiness.

What should have been a romantic happy time, was quickly turning into a sad moment. I wanted to be happy but something deep inside of me just would not let me get happy. Instead of happiness I was depressed. I should have been ecstatic but deep down I was sad; really sad. As much as I loved Mike, doubt started arising in me.

I kneeled down beside Mike in the sand, "Don't do this now, I'm not ready for this!"

Mike looked up at me with his eyes asking me *why?*

Before he could say anything, I continued. "Mike, I have truly enjoyed us taking things slow and spending time together; however, we can't just pretend like the last couple months didn't happen. You have two outside kids now and a baby momma that will stop at nothing to win you over and on many occasions you have already proved that you're weak for her. I don't want to have to wonder if you are still messing with her every time you go see your kids or pick them up and drop them off.

"If that's how you feel, Tammie you can go with me to Rachel's house. I'll do whatever I have to do to prove to you that it is really over between me and Rachel," Mike said sincerely.

"That may be true, but words are just words until you put them in action. I'm sorry but now is just not a good time for us to consider remarrying," I said sternly and walked back toward the room.

After a few minutes, Mike came back into the room with a plastic bag filled with the candles and rose petals.

"I'm sorry, Tammie. I shouldn't have asked you to marry me again. I know I got a lot of making up to do. So can I at least take you to dinner?" He asked me.

"Sure just let me call my mom and check on the kids and then I'll call Sharon and Nicole and see if they want to meet us for dinner.

My mom finally picked up on the fourth ring.

"Hey momma, how are you?" I said cheerfully as if I hadn't been crying minutes earlier.

"I'm fine, baby. I'd be okay if my grandbabies didn't talk so much. You enjoying Hawaii? I bet it is beautiful," my mom said.

"Hawaii is beautiful, Ma. It's really nice here. How are the kids? They are not giving you any trouble are they?" I asked in my motherly tone.

"Girl I got this! I raised five kids and ten grandchildren before yours were even thought about, so don't try to play me. If you think I'm incapable of watching the kids then you and that husband of yours should hop back on that plane and come get your children," my mom said to me in her serious tone.

"Momma, I'm sorry. I didn't mean to offend you. Anyway, I just was checking on you guys and I will bring you all something back," I said.

"Okay Tammie, take care of yourself and watch your back, you know I still don't trust that husband of yours for all I know he can be taking you around the world to kill you," my mom said in a very serious tone.

"Okay momma. Love you and I'll talk to you later. Don't worry about me, I'll be okay. Kiss my babies for me! Mwah!"

I got off the phone with my mom and immediately called Sharon to invite her and Nicole to have dinner with us. Sharon and Nicole was already down near the dining hall, so they agreed to wait around until we were ready.

Mike was in the shower when I got off the phone. Stripping naked, I quickly joined Mike in the shower. Mike started kissing my body and washing me, but my mind was on a million things except having sex. I ignored his advances and he eventually got the picture.

I quickly washed my body again and got out the shower. I wrapped a towel around me and laid across the bed starting up at the ceiling. Before I could get my thoughts together, Mike phone started to buzz.

I ignored the phone but after two missed calls a text message came in. I grabbed Mike's phone to see who it was. As expected it was Rachel. I hastily deleted Rachel's calls.

I opened up the text and begin to read it, *Mike something is wrong with the twins. It looks like an allergic reaction to something. I'm on my way to the hospital now! Please call me ASAP!*

I didn't believe Rachel. She was always trying to get Mike to come over and I bet this was just another one of her lies. I bet she found out about our vacation and just want to interrupt things.

I'm not going to let Rachel ruin our vacation so I deleted the message as well, put Mike's phone back where he left it and started getting dressed.

I didn't tell Mike about the calls and text from Rachel. We finished getting dressed and left for dinner.

When we got downstairs Sharon and Nicole was waiting on us in the lobby. Sharon had this look on her face like she was angry at someone but she didn't want it to show.

"Mike, can I talk to you for a minute, please?" Sharon asked.

"Sure, no problem," Mike responded while moving to the side with Sharon.

I saw Sharon pull out her phone and show him some text messages. My heart skipped a beat. *What if Rachel texted her? What if the twins are really sick? What will Mike do when he finds out I deleted his stuff off his phone.* I was getting real uneasy trying to read Mike's face as he read whatever was on Sharon's phone.

Mike gave Sharon her phone and immediately pulled out his phone and called someone. He had a look on his face that said I'm mad but concerned at the same time.

Sharon walked back over to Nicole and me.

"Nicole, can you give me a minute alone with Tammie," Sharon demanded.

As soon as Nicole walked off, Sharon dove right in.

"How could you Tammie?"

"How could I what?" I responded.

Sharon retorted, "Why would you go through Mike's phone and not tell him Rachel called and texted him?!"

"I thought she was lying because she is always doing stuff like that!" I countered.

"Well, she wasn't lying! The twins are in the hospital and it's serious Tammie! How could you do that? You better hope Mike forgives you and that those babies are okay because if anything happens he is going to blame you for not telling him," Sharon exclaimed and walked off into the dining area with Nicole right behind her leaving me standing their alone.

I started to walk towards Mike but he just walked pass me and headed in the direction of our room, still on the phone. I stood in the lobby for a while more. I didn't know whether to go to the room and face Mike or just let him be.

I went back to the room to and by the time I got there, Mike was off the phone and packing up the few things he had unpacked. I didn't say anything to him and he didn't say anything to me. He was off the phone now and I could see that he was pissed at me, but most of all, he was hurt.

Even though he hurt me when he conceived those twins, I would never do anything to purposely hurt those babies. I should have never answered his phone. My momma always said if you go looking for something then you will find what you looking for.

My curiosity got the best of me and as much as I said I wanted our marriage to work, deep down I didn't trust Mike. I could never trust him around Rachel again.

Rachel has a hold on Mike. It's something about her that he just can't seem to shake and with her having his babies, they will always be connected and now I'm almost certain that my marriage to him will never work.

I was so deep into my thoughts that I almost missed Mike going out the door with his bags. I hopped in front of the door blocking it.

"Where do you think you are going Mike?" I yelled.

"Tammie, I am not about to argue with you. My babies are sick and I want to be there for them. If it were our children, you would expect me to be there. Those are my boys and I am GOING to be there for them. Considering what you did, I think it's best if you don't come to the hospital, I don't need you and Rachel getting into it."

I opened my mouth to say something but he stopped me before I could say anything.

"What you did was childish and unnecessary. If you couldn't get over the fact that I had kids with her, then I should have never been here with you. You don't want me, you just want to win. You just didn't want to lose me to her. It was all a game to you. I know I fucked up Tammie, but I was sincere when I said I wanted to work on our marriage. Anyway, I got to go, I need some time alone to think so maybe you can just fly back with Sharon and Nicole in the morning. I'll call you when I can," he replied and walked out the door with his bags.

I wanted to go after him, but I couldn't. It was as if I was stuck in the spot where I sat. I knew I had to let him go. I should have been let him go, but he was right. I was holding on to him for all the wrong reasons. It wasn't because I still loved him and wanted our marriage to work. I just didn't want him to be with Rachel. I didn't want her to win.

Somehow I convinced myself that I actually did want this marriage to work. Maybe it was the kids, or maybe it was the history we share, but deep down I knew. I knew I could never trust him again and I knew that I wasn't over the fact that he betrayed me with someone I considered a friend.

It's hard to trust someone the second time around after they have already given you a reason not to trust them. Yes, I was wrong for answering his phone and deleting his calls and texts but my actions were reactions to all the bullshit and drama that he put me through.

I continue justifying my actions, in my head. Wondering why was I staying in a marriage that was without a doubt, *irretrievably broken*. I knew what I had to do regardless of how the situation with Rachel and the twins played out.

I called Sharon and told her I was going to be leaving Hawaii tonight.

"Hey Sharon, I'm leaving tonight. I'm sorry if I ruined your trip but you and Nicole should stay a few more days because you deserve this break. So stay and enjoy yourself and I will keep you informed of the situation back home."

"Okay, Tammie. I'm sorry for snapping on you but you were the one always keeping us on the straight and narrow and now you are doing some of the same things you always telling us not to do in a relationship. I don't want to argue with you. You are my friend and I love you. I will always have your back but you really need to analyze things and figure out if staying in your marriage is best for you. Have a safe trip back and call me as soon as you know something," she said.

"I will girl and thanks again for the trip, sorry I couldn't stay long," I responded.

I packed my bags and cleaned up the room as best I could. I checked out the hotel and caught a cab to the airport. As luck would have it, Mike and I ended up on the same flight. After I put up my carry-ons. I went over to where Mike was seated.

"Mike, I know you still mad at me. I just want to say I'm sorry. I never should have invaded your privacy by going through your phone and I never should have agreed to work on our marriage when I knew I wasn't over what happened. You were right. I couldn't bear losing to her. Anyway, just wanted to say I'm sorry."

I expected him to say something or to even fuss at me, yell, or scream or something but he didn't. He ignored me as if I was a stranger. I knew he was still mad at me so I just got up and went back to my seat.

The flight back to Atlanta seemed longer and sadder. Every mile closer to home, the knot in my stomach grew bigger and bigger. I became nauseated and if I wasn't so afraid to move on the plane, I would have been ran to the restroom and puked my guts out. I was finally able to sleep, so that took my mind off my nervousness of flying and thoughts about the situation between Mike and myself.

I awoke just as the captain was announcing that we were landing. Glancing down at my watch, I saw it was only a little after nine in the morning.

After exiting the plane and getting my luggage, I didn't bother trying to find Mike to talk to him or to ride home with him and going to the hospital was not a good idea. So, I caught a cab home, showered, and got in the bed. I didn't want to talk to anyone. I just wanted to sleep.

5

MIKE

Tammie and I ended up on the same plane departing Hawaii. She came over and tried to apologize but I wasn't trying to hear her. I never would have expected Tammie to act like that. I know that I am partly to blame for her insecurities but I thought we were starting over and actually going to work on our marriage. Even if she didn't believe Rachel, she should have told me.

My mind was racing and so many what if situations played in my head, I tried to sleep but the entire time my mind kept wondering. Once we landed in Atlanta, I grabbed my bags and headed straight to the hospital.

"Can you tell me what room Mikye and Mikele Dawson is in?" I asked the old lady sitting behind the welcome desk.

"It looks like they are in the NICU..."

I ran to the elevators before she can finished.

"Third floor young man!" She yelled out to me. The elevator came and as I entered I said a prayer in my head for God to watch over my boys.

When I entered the NICU waiting room, Rachel ran into my arms as tears poured down her face. She tried to tell me what happened but I couldn't comprehend anything she said because she was crying so hard.

Persia came up to me and decoded what Rachel was trying to tell me. I didn't even see Persia when I came in.

"The twins had some type of allergic reaction to the baby formula and stopped breathing. They are stable for now, but it's still touch and go and we can only see them like every four hours. The next visitation is coming up at 12," Persia whispered. I looked at my watched and realized, I still had an hour or so before I could see the boys and talk to the doctor.

My knees got weak and I quickly walked, with Rachel, to the nearest seats and sat down. Rachel took the seat next to me, but once again, buried her face in my chest sobbing hysterically.

"I'm going to get some air and give you guys some time alone," Persia said woefully with tears in her eyes as well. The way they both looked, the situations with my boys were serious.

Although, I wanted to cry as loud as Rachel, I had to be strong for her. I got up and got her some tissue to clean her face.

"I got here as fast as I could. I'm sorry I didn't get your messages sooner, but I'm here now and I'm not going anywhere," I said.

Rachel must was tired because she drifted off to sleep for a while. I reclined the chair back for her and allowed her to rest a while, until it was visitation hour.

Persia came back from downstairs. She had regained her composure and was looking like herself again.

"Where's Tammie? She asked me. When Persia said Tammie's name, I got angry all over again. I started to just ignore Persia but she was looking directly at me, waiting on me to answer.

"At home I guess?" I replied with venom in my voice. Persia wanted to ask another question but she didn't. She just picked up her phone and called Tammie.

While she talked to Tammie, I went to the restroom. I had no interest in speaking with Tammie or trying to see where she was or what she was doing. I was still pissed at her for what she did.

Persia told me she was leaving and that she would call back to check on the boys later. I'm sure she was going to check on Tammie. They were really close, so I'm sure Tammie told her what happened between us.'

When I came back from the restroom, it was almost visiting hour, so I woke Rachel up. It Time was dragging by and it seems to take forever for the clock to strike twelve.

Finally it was twelve and the doors were unlocked. Rachel and I washed our hands at the check in station to the NICU and put on the required gown before entering the room. My heart was about to jump out of my chest, I was so scared. As we got closer, Rachel slowed down and pointed to the room door, signaling for me to go first.

I said a short prayer in my head and walked into the room. I almost bolted out of the room when I saw the boys hooked up to so many machines. It literally broke my heart. Tears filled my eyes and leaked out before I could wipe them away, but I didn't care.

Even though the twins were only a month old and I hadn't bonded that much with them, I was still their father and my heart was aching for them. Seeing their tiny bodies filled with tubes would make even the strongest man break down.

I was so fixated on the twins that I didn't even notice the nurse on the other side of the room.

"Hello. I'm Debbie and I'm going to be the boys nurse until 7," she said.

"Hello. Can you tell us what's going on with the boys? Are they stable?" I asked nervously.

"I'll have the doctor come in," she said as she rapidly excited the room.

A few nerve-wrecking moments later, the doctor came into the room. Up until now Rachel was standing between the two beds that the twins were in. When she saw the doctor, she immediately sat down. The look on his face made me want to sit down too, but I just moved closer to the chair that Rachel sat in.

"Good evening. I'm Dr. Robinson."

"Evening Doctor, I'm Michael Dawson, the twins' father. I just got in from a trip can you tell me what is going on with my boys?"

"Nice to meet you Mr. Dawson, and I'm sorry that it has to be under these circumstances. Your twins are suffering from a bacterial infection called *cronobacter sakazakii* or *enterobacter sakazakii*. This type of infection is sometimes associated with an allergic reaction to infant formula. Even though we have identified what it is, we are still concerned about the twins because their bodies are not reacting to the antibiotics as we would like. Because of that the infection is spreading and making them sicker. We are doing the very best we can to get them better because the longer they have this infection, the greater the risk of them going into epileptic shock or the risk of the infection turning into meningitis. We are starting them on stronger antibiotics to try to attack the infection more effectively and we have them on round-the-clock care, meaning a nurse will be present in the room with them at all time to monitor them. Now, Mr. Dawson, I'm going to be honest with you, this type of infection is very rare and potentially dangerous. Once again, we are doing everything we possibly can to take care of your babies," Dr. Robinson said and quickly left the room.

As soon as he left, I completely broke down. I tried to be strong for Rachel, but realization of how serious the situation was started a waterfall on my face that I could not stop. I walked over between the two beds and I laid one hand on Mikye and one hand on Mikele and prayed to God to please heal my babies.

When I was done praying, I walked back over to Rachel.

"Have you eaten today, Rachel?"

"No, I'm not hungry. I just want my boys to be okay," she said to me with more tears in her eyes.

"Rachel, you can't help them if you are in the hospital yourself for dehydration and starvation. You have to keep your strength up for them. Here's some money. Go get you something to eat and check on your other children and I'll stay here with the boys for a while. I'll text you if anything changes," I said assuredly.

Rachel hesitated to go, but she finally mustered up the strength to go and get her something to eat. I texted Persia and Sharon to give them an update on the twins. I knew Persia would in turn tell Tammie. Nicole texted back and let me know that her and Nicole would be leaving Hawaii in a few hours. Persia didn't text me back.

Debbie entered the room and changed the boys' diapers and got their temperature. She also checked the machines and recorded the readings.

"The twins have a slight fever and their blood pressure is still kind of low, but everything else is looking okay. Visiting hours is over in five minutes. You can either wait in the NICU waiting room or you can talk to the receptionist desk to see if any of the family rooms are available."

I was about to ask her what is a family room but she must have read my mind and answered for me.

"Family rooms are rooms that the family of NICU or ICU patients can rent to get some sleep. So basically it's kind of like a hotel room that allows you to be closer to your loved one, she said preparing to leave.

"Thank you Debbie and thank you for taking care of my boys," I said.

"You're welcome," she said and left the room.

I kneeled close to Mikele and whispered to him, "I love you Mikele and turned and whispered the same thing to Mikye. Then I said another prayer for them both before leaving the room.

I stopped by the nurse's station and got a family room for Rachel, so that she could sleep there instead of on the big recliners in the waiting room.

I didn't see Rachel, so I texted her phone to see had she gone home. Rachel texted back and let me know she was in the chapel.

I reached the chapel and found Rachel sitting in the fourth pew, in a daze. I called her name twice and it was as if she didn't hear me. I called her name a little louder and she jumped!

"I'm sorry, I didn't mean to scare you. I just wanted to check on you and make sure you are okay," I whispered as I sat down beside her. I got you a family room you can sleep in when you stay at the hospital, so you don't have to sleep in the waiting room," I said.

"Thanks," She said barely looking up at me. Her eyes were bloodshot red and small bags of stress were forming underneath them with a trail of tears that feel from her eyes into her lap, yet it didn't deter from her beauty. Rachel was still beautiful and the tears that fell from her eyes made me see her in an entirely different light.

I no longer saw the desperate, devious, man-struck Rachel. I saw a mother. A mother that would do anything to save her children. I can't remember much of my time around Rachel, before her and I hooked up, but the times I do remember, she was always a great mother. After all the drama, her backstabbing ways and devious behavior, overshadowed her image as a good mother, but now I was seeing it again.

"The boys are fighters. Doctor said they are getting a little better, but they aren't out of the woods yet. So, we just got to continue to pray for them," I told Rachel. She didn't say a word, just laid her head on my shoulder. I kissed Rachel on her forehead. I'm not sure if I did it because I wanted to comfort her or if it was my body's natural reaction to a woman lying her head on my chest.

By the time I realized what I had done, it was too late. Rachel and I was kissing passionately before breaking apart. No matter how I try to deny it, maybe just maybe I fell for Rachel like she fell for me. Any other time, I would have pushed her away from me, but considering everything that is going on, we both needed a shoulder to lean on.

I lifted Rachel's face up to mines and glazed into her big brown eyes that were still red from crying. A lone tear escaped the corner of her eye and I wiped it with my fingers. She closed her eyes to stop me from looking into her eyes and reading the desires of her heart and the secrets within her soul. I pulled her close to me and kissed her.

The door to the chapel opened and the light from the corridor broke our kiss. Rachel and I both looked towards the door. All I could mutter was, "Oh shit!"

6

SHARON

Nicole and I made it back to Atlanta and went straight to the hospital. We stayed in Hawaii an extra night to get a little time in together, but her husband kept calling and texting and ruined everything. Every time he called, she became guilty that she was here with me and I was reminded that she didn't belong to me.

We ended up arguing and she went to the bar at the hotel. I thought she would eventually come back, so we could make up, but she stayed out all night. I can't say for sure, if she was with someone else, but I'm almost certain she was.

I don't know if she was with someone else or not and I didn't ask her. She gave me the silent treatment and I did the same. We didn't talk the entire flight home.

I know Nicole loves me, but I also know that she loves her husband. I'm not sure if Nicole is gay or bisexual and whenever I bring the subject up, she cuts the conversation short. She always says, *none of that matters, just know that I love you, Sharon!*

I haven't given my heart to anyone since Mont and I divorced, out of fear of getting my heart broke. The fact that I fell for a woman with a husband, a husband who's a police officer, was absolutely crazy.

"Hello. Can you tell me what room Mikele and Mikye Dawson is in?" I asked the old lady sitting behind the welcome counter.

"They are in the NICU on the third floor. Just stop by the nurses' desk on that floor and someone will help you further," she said.

"Thank you," I said as Nicole and I headed to the elevators. She was still giving me the silent treatment but right now my mind wasn't really on her and our issues. My mind was on Rachel and her babies. I said a short prayer in my head as we stepped off the elevators and walked into the NICU waiting room.

I didn't see Rachel or Mike anywhere in the waiting room, so Nicole and I sat down to wait on them. While we were waiting a bunch of police officers came into the waiting area. They all had worried looks on their faces. When Nicole looked up and saw the officers, she started freaking out. Then it donned on me that her husband was a police officer.

"Calm down, Nicole. You don't know if it's him or not," I said grabbing and holding her. "I'll go over and ask one of the nurses, just calm down. Okay?"

I walked to the nurses' station and asked if she knew what happened and why there was so many officers here. She stated that an officer was shot during a traffic stop, but she couldn't tell me his name. I thanked her for telling and walked back over to Nicole.

"An officer was shot during a traffic jam, but she wouldn't tell me his name," I told Nicole. Nicole started freaking out.

"Calm down, Nicole. Try calling him and see if he answer," I instructed her.

She took out her phone to call her husband. At the same time that Nicole was on the phone, somebody's phone on the other side of the waiting room starting ringing loudly.

Nicole started looking around the waiting room. She and her husband must have spotted each other at the same time because they both had looks of surprise on their face. As if I wasn't even sitting there, Nicole got up and ran into her husband's arms.

As I watched him kiss her and whisper in her ear and how she responded to his kisses and his touch pissed me off. She said she didn't love him, but her body was snitching on her real bad. That kiss said more than *I thought you were hurt,* that kiss said *I love you too and I missed you.* She really forgot about me when she saw him. Like I didn't even exist. I started to make a scene but instead I just got up to leave. I clearly was not needed nor wanted at the moment.

***

As I was passing by the hospital chapel, I heard noises coming from inside, I peeped in to check it out.

As soon as I entered, I wish I hadn't. Rachel and Tammie was inside fighting while Mike was doing his best to break them up. Every time, Mike managed to break them apart, one would reach over and hit the other one or hit Mike.

Tammie's been through a lot, but she was dead wrong for deleting Rachel's calls and text to Mike, so I didn't say anything. Like a movie-goer sneaking into a movie theater, I took a seat in the back and watched the fight.

Mike pulled the duo apart once again and this time, Tammie reached over and punched Rachel. Before Tammie could disconnect the punch, Rachel had grabbed a fist full of her hair with one hand was trying to connect her other hand with Tammie face. Mike moved out the way after one of Rachel's blows hit him and the duo was going head to head.

They were giving and taking punches. At times it seemed that Rachel was winning and at times it seemed that Tammie was winning. Surprisingly no one fell. As they started to get tired, Rachel locked her hands in Tammie's head and Tammie locked hers in Rachel. Once again, Mike was trying to break them apart. I finally decided to intervene. I pulled Rachel off Tammie and helped Mike keep them separate.

After about five minutes of twisting and shouting, the two were separated. Mike told Tammie to go home because her being at the hospital would only keep up mess and that this is not about her but his boys instead. Then he turned to Rachel and told her to let it go and focus on the boys.

Tammie didn't leave right away. She planted herself on the end of the pew and refused to leave. Mike didn't try to force her though. He just grabbed Rachel's hand and they walked out of the chapel together.

Now, I know he was upset about what Rachel did, but I didn't see that one coming. That simple act of affection, broke Tammie down. Either she was in shock and couldn't respond or she didn't want to give them the satisfaction of seeing her break down. It was the latter, because as soon as the door closed, she fell apart. I had never in my life seen Tammie break down like that.

I quickly texted Persia to come to the hospital to be with Tammie. Tammie and I were close, but she and Persia were closer. I sat beside Tammie and just held her.

"It's going to be okay, Tammie. You just got to give him some time to process this. He's just angry. That's all."

Tammie tried to respond back, but I couldn't understand what she was saying because her cries were drowning out her words. My phone started vibrating in my pocket which broke the embrace between Tammie and me. Tammie used that time to get herself together, while I checked my phone.

Persia texted me that she would come as soon as she could but she was dealing with something with Derek and she would text me back when she was on her way. I texted her back okay.

"Tammie, I think it's best if you just go back home. Mike is upset and Rachel wants to kill you. This is not the time or place to deal with the issues between you guys. Right now that is not what's important. We all should be focused on the boys getting better. I'll keep you updated as much as possible," I suggested.

"Ok...Ok...I'm leaving," she replied back.

"Are you okay to drive?"

"Yea, I'm fine. I'll be okay," Tammie stated and grabbed her things and left.

I stayed in the chapel and said a prayer for the boys before going back to the waiting room where Mike and Rachel was and to see what Nicole was doing.

***

I wasn't prepared for what I saw when I walked back into the waiting room. Rachel and Mike was kissing and I'm not talking just a peck on the cheek. They were so engrossed in the kiss that they didn't even see me, so I stepped back out into the hallway.

By the time I re-entered the waiting area, they had stopped kissing. I sat down besides Rachel and Mike and I could see the nervousness on both their faces.

"Rachel, any updates on the boys?" I asked.

"Not really, we won't really know anything until the next visitation," Rachel replied softly.

Mike excused himself and left out of the waiting room. I looked over at Nicole and she looked down as if she didn't know me. I didn't expect her to blow her cover and let her husband know about us, but I at least expected her to at least acknowledge that I exist. Make eye contact or sneak a text or something to let me know I'm not in this alone. The truth of the matter is that I am in this alone. I realize that more than ever. I fell for *somebody else's wife*, so it was nobody's fault but my own.

"I'll be right back, Rachel. I think I see an old friend," I said.

I walked over to where Nicole and Brian sat.

"Nicole? I thought that were you... How are you doing? How you been?" I said pretending as if I was an old friend.

Nicole looked surprised that I actually came over, but she played along. "Sharon, I'm ok. I'm here with my husband, Brian. His friend, Chico was shot during a traffic stop. What are you doing here?" She asked me as if she didn't already now.

"I'm here with my friend, Rachel. Her twin boys had a severe reaction to baby formula and they are in the NICU."

Brian looked as if he wanted to ask me something but instead he told Nicole that he would give us some time to catch up and he left.

Once Nicole was sure that Brian was gone, she started apologizing. "I'm so sorry, Sharon. I just couldn't tell him about us. Not here, not right now, especially when his best friend is fighting for his life. I'm going to tell him, I promise, but now just isn't the time," she said to me.

I simply replied, "Ok Nicole. I'll give you some time to work that out. I'll talk to you later and I got up and left her sitting there. When I walked into the hallway, I saw Rachel and Nicole's husband talking to each other as if they knew each other. When I walked up, Brian walked off.

"Rachel, I'm exhausted. I was trying to wait until visitation, but this jetlag is wearing on me, please keep me updated about the boys. I'll be back, once I get some rest. Hang in there and call me if there is any changes. I'll talk to you later," I said and left.

I'm sure Nicole would text me later, but for the moment, I didn't want to hear from her, so I turned my phone off and headed home.

7

NICOLE

Watching Sharon leave out of that waiting room, upset and hurt, made me feel so bad. I saw the disappointing look on her face when she stormed out after witnessing Brian and I kissing.

Brian does not know about Sharon and I couldn't risk him finding out about her, even if it meant hurting her. I would make it up to her later and hopefully she would understand and forgive me.

I know Sharon is ready for us to be an official couple, but we can't right now because Brian and I are still married. Brian knows I'm attracted to women, but he has no idea that I've actually acted upon that attraction.

Before Sharon, I was with a lot of women. The night I met Sharon, I thought it was going to be another one night stand, but something happened and I just couldn't leave her alone.

It wasn't just the sex, her genuine spirit and caring personality was intriguing. Normally after sex, I would get up and go, but with Sharon, I didn't want to leave.

She knew about my husband and she was fine with that until, she started falling in love with me, then everything changed.

I really do love Sharon, but part of me still loves my husband as well.

Now, she gets upset whenever she's around and Brian call or if I say I have to go home or that Brian and I have something planned, it's an argument.

The short time we were in Hawaii was horrible. We didn't have sex or make love not once. She got an attitude every time my phone rang or vibrated.

Even though, I ignored most of Brian's calls on the trip, that still wasn't enough to make her happy. We would still end up arguing.

Our last night in Hawaii, she was upset about the situation with Tammie, Rachel, and Mike. She wanted to talk about that situation and I wanted no parts of that conversation. I just wanted us to enjoy our last night together.

Just when it seemed like we were going to enjoy ourselves and have some fun on the island, Brian called and Sharon flipped out. She started going on and on about how she is tired of sharing me and how I need to make up my mind what I wanted to do and who I wanted.

I hate being told what I need to do and when to do it, so I stormed out of the room and left her there, alone. I went to the bar and ended up having a one-night stand with a woman, I met in the bar.

I was sitting at the bar drowning my sorrows with shots of Patron. By the fifth shot, a lady came over and sat next to me.

"You know, when you wake up in the morning, the pain is still going to be there!" She stated to me.

"Well, until tomorrow, this Patron is going to be my temporary fix," I replied without even looking up at her.

"Tequila will help you forget, but it can also create other problems," the lady commented.

I really didn't feel like talking and she was getting on my nerves. Finally, I looked up at her and I was immediately speechless. She was exquisite!

Her skin was the color of honey. She had light ash brown dreadlocks with light reddish brown highlights with chestnut colored eyes. She was curvaceous because her hips and ass spilled over the barstool. She wore a sleeveless, black midi party dress

"And what kind of problems can tequila create?" I asked staring in her eyes.

"The kind where you wake up in a strange place and don't remember what you did and who you did it with," she said with a laugh. "I'm sorry, I'm just fucking with you. My name is Zuri and your name is?" She said while extending her hand out, so I could shake it.

"My name is Nicole," I answered as I quickly shook and released her hand. "Your dreads are gorgeous! Can I touch them?"

"No! Only time I like people to touch my hair is when we fucking!" Zuri said laughing harder. I'm sorry you make this really easy. You really should loosen up some. I won't bite I promise, unless you want me to."

"Nice to know you are a comedian at my expense, but anyway nice to meet you," I replied.

"Likewise. Let me buy you a drink, so I can show you that I'm truly sorry and that I want to get to know you."

"Okay, fine, but just so you know, I require at least a two-drink minimum!" I said laughing.

"There it is! I knew it had to be a beautiful smile to match such a beautiful lady!"

Zuri was definitely flirting with me and I was definitely enjoying it. It had been a long time since that happened.

After many more Patron shots, good conversation, and slick bots of sarcastic jokes, I ended up in Zuri's room with her. I was a little tipsy, but I wouldn't say I was drunk. I wanted Zuri just as much as she wanted me.

I started to kiss her and she stopped me.

"Don't kiss me," she said and then she kissed me long, hard, and deep.

When our lips finally separated, I said, "So, I can't kiss you, but you can kiss me, huh? Well, what can I do?"

She replied with a smile, "Nothing. I don't want you to do anything. Tonight is going to be all about me pleasing you. So take off all your clothes and follow me into the bath!"

Zuri left and went into the bathroom. I heard water running, so I did as she asked and took off my clothes.

I've always been the aggressive one in one night stands and to watch someone else do to me, what I have done to some many others felt extraordinary, yet it turned me on in a way I haven't been in a long time.

When I walked in the bathroom, Zuri had drawn us a nice warm bubble with a few candles lit on the sink.

I was speechless. I never had a one-night stand like this before and I never put this much effort into my one-night stands, but Zuri was different. I figured out that much during our conversations at the bar.

As if reading my mind, she said, "Relax, I'm not trying marry you, I just want to please you, now get in!

I guess I didn't move fast enough for her, because she walked over me and kissed me again. This time she kissed me from my lips to my ears, to my neck and on to my breasts. Her soft lips on my nipples were building a fire within me that ion think water could have put out.

I grabbed the back of her head with one hand and forced her mouth to make love to my breasts, while guiding her hand to my drenched pussy.

"Oh, baby! You're so wet for me!" she muttered.

Breaking her lips from my breasts and kissing down my chest. She grabbed my pelvic area and thrusted her tongue between my super soaked lips and I melted into her. She licked up and down my pussy until my sweet nectar covered her tongue, before standing up and kissing me on the neck as she whispered in my ear for me to get in the tub.

I tried to kiss her again, but she prevented me. I got into the tub and she grabbed the Caress body wash and a bath sponge and preceded to bathe me.

After she has finished bathing me, I stepped out the tub and started drying off. Zuri stopped me and finished drying me off and started applying lotion to my skin. Her touch was almost as lethal as her kisses, yet she still wouldn't let me do anything to her.

This woman was breaking down every wall I had ever put up. I am not the submissive type, but for Zuri, I was submitting to her in ways, I never even knew I could submit to someone.

"Lie on your stomach on the bed!"

There was no point in protesting at this point. It felt amazing have someone cater to me.

I laid on my stomach and Zuri lubricated my body from my neck to my heel. Then she began giving me a back massage, while occasionally planting kisses up and down my back.

"Get on your knees and bend over!" Zuri demanded.

I hesitated a little, but once again, I did as I was told. Deep down, I was kind of enjoying being bossed around like that. I guess that's how the women I used to be with felt when I made them submit to me.

Once I was bend over, Zuri kissed from my shoulders blades to my ass cheeks. Then she parted my ass with her hands and licked up and down my ass. I never had that done before and that shit felt so good that it made my pussy squirt.

Zuri inside two fingers inside of me and massaged my clit, while still licking up and down the crack of my ass. I couldn't focus from all the pleasure I was feeling. I lost count of how many times she made me cum. The smallest touch from her forced a reaction out of me.

After the last orgasm, Zuri got up. "Get up!" She commanded me. Call me a lame or whatever, but Zuri was definitely training my ass and the way she was doing it was so awesome that I willingly submitted to her with a smile.

When I got up, Zuri started back kissing me. She kissed from my lips, ears, neck, and breasts, and back up again.

She whispered in my ear, "Come sit on my face!"

Zuri laid on the bed and I straddled her in the sign of the cancer. I wanted to at least taste her once before our night together ended, but when she saw what I was trying to do she stopped me and signaled for me to turn around the other way.

I turned around and moved up until my pussy sat near her lips. I lifted up a little and held on to the headboard as she feasted on me.

Each orgasm got bigger and more intense and the more I tried to move to stop my body from convulsing, the deeper she licked and sucked. After my umpteenth orgasm, she finally let up and I was able to climb off her face and lay on the bed. Before I knew what hit me I was asleep.

I awoke around a few hours later, Zuri was still asleep. I gathered my clothes and shoes, quickly put them on and left.

When I made it back to the room Sharon and I shared, I saw that she had already packed her bags. She pretended to be asleep but I know she wasn't sleep.

I felt bad for what I allowed to happen between Zuri and myself, but was it really cheating if I didn't do anything but allow her to please me?

Knowing Sharon, I know she would see me talking to another woman as cheating, so there was no way I was ever going to tell her about Zuri. Matter of fact, I don't even know Zuri's last name so the odds of me running into her again were astronomical.

I hopped in the shower and washed all evidence of Zuri away. Even though I washed away the physical evidence of Zuri on me, the memories were forever etched in my head.

I have never had a one night stand like that. I have never submitted to anyone like that, not even Sharon. It's a good thing, I don't know much about Zuri because the effect she had on me could become addictive.

That one-night with her has played over and over in my head like a song on repeat. It awoke feelings and urges, I hadn't had in a long time.

Sharon was still mad at me for staying out all night in Hawaii and when I left for the trip, Brian and I wasn't on the best terms. I decided to plan a special evening for Brian.

I cooked steak and shrimp with a creamy garlic butter sauce with parsley potatoes and homemade macaroni & cheese, yeast rolls, and made a Caesar salad. For dessert, I made his favorite—a double layer strawberry cake with strawberry icing topped with real strawberries.

I finished dinner, set the table, made our plates and put them in the oven to keep them warm until Brian came home. Then I went upstairs and changed into a white lace negligee with white thongs and red stilettos.

When I heard Brian pull in the driveway, I quickly lit the candles and dimmed the lights. I stood a few inches from the door, so that I would be the first thing he saw when he opened the door.

After a minute or so, Brian unlocked the door and walked in.

"Welcome home, Baby!" I shouted.

Even though, Brian had been at work; he looked so handsome. The low fade with the afro top and tapered sides hair cut fit his face completely. With his coco skin, dark eyes, wide smile, and deep dimples, the haircut just screamed sexy! It gave him a college boy look. His haircut also highlighted his natural hair texture. Instead of the usual low cut all around, having his hair tapered on the sides allowed his hair to grow, which caused his curls became more and more defined. The white V-neck t-shirt he wore showed off his progress of hitting the gym.

For a minute, it was almost like I was seeing Brian in an entirely different light. I walked to him and kissed him, while running my fingers through his hair. At that moment, all I could think about was the love I had for this man and wondering how could I ever just completely let him go.

8

RACHEL

"Lord, please help me! I need a miracle right now. My boys needs a miracle. Please don't punish them for what I've done. I'm sorry. Please spare my children. Please Jesus, I promise I will change. Just save my children," I prayed in my head over and over again since the doctor gave us an update on the boys.

It's been almost a week and my boys were still in the NICU. The doctor wanted to move them to a children's hospital but they were too weak to even move. His words keep echoing in my ear like a pesky fly that won't go away.

"The antibiotics are no longer working. The infection is spreading and things just aren't looking good. Their bodies are too small to fight this type of infection. We need a miracle, right now. This infection is very aggressive and the medicines available to infants simply is not working and all other medication is simply too strong for their young bodies and could cause organ failure or seizures even if given in small doses. All we can do right now is *pray*. I want you to know I'm doing the best I can to make them comfortable but that's really all I can do right now unless something else changes," the doctor told us and left out of the room.

Just watching my babies, I couldn't do anything but cry. I couldn't help but think this is my fault. God is punishing me for wrecking Tammie and Mike's marriage. This is my payback. This is my Karma. These are the results of the seeds I have been sowing.

I could see my babies slipping away from me. They were losing weight and now they were sleeping longer and harder to wake up. According to the doctor, neither was a good sign.

As I stood between the beds that held my babies, looking from one to the other, Michael came behind me and wrapped his arm around me. Lately, we have been letting our emotions get the best of us and give us this false sense of reality, like we should be together when in fact, we shouldn't be near each other at all.

"Get away from me, Mike!" I yelled but immediately brought my voice down upon remembering where I was. "Don't you see that our kids are suffering because of the decisions we made. You are a married man and even though we have kids together, that does not give you a pass to make out or be intimate together. Please don't touch, kiss, hug, or rub me anymore. We have done enough damage and created enough chaos with this crazy affair or whatever you want to call it. Go home to Tammie. Forgive her. Stop using what she did as an excuse to get with me. It isn't right and I will no longer be a part of that. Tammie has never done anything but try to help me and I messed that up. She had every reason to act the way she did. If anything happens to the boys, don't blame her. Maybe I shouldn't blame myself either, maybe it's all been a part of his plan. I don't want to lose my boys, but I know I can't argue with God's will. All I can do is pray. There's nothing you can do here, just go home and if anything changes, I'll let you know as soon as possible."

"Okay, Rachel. If that's what you want. For the record, we have something. It may not be love, but it's more than us being parents, too. I do love my wife, but I also feel something for you that I can't explain. It's like a moth to a flame, when we are near each other, it's like I just lose control. I've tried so hard to bury the feelings I have for you, but something keeps pulling me back to you. I'll respect your decision. Maybe you are right. Maybe God is punishing US for everything we did to Tammie. We conceived our children in lust, in sin, and now God is punishing them for our actions," Mike said becoming overwhelmed with emotions.

Tears started flooding down Mike's face. "I'll talk to you later, please keep me updated if anything changes," he said and walked out of the room.

I sat in the chair and continued to pray for a miracle until the nurse came in to tell me that visitation was over. I whispered, *mommy loves you* to the boys and kissed them.

I should be going home, but I just couldn't bear to be away from them and something happened. I couldn't have that on my conscious, so I headed back to the family room, Mike rented for me.

On the way back to the room, I was so busy checking my phone that I ran directly into someone. "You need to walk with your head up before you run into the wrong person!" The man said. I started to snap, but when I looked up, he just laughed.

"I'm sorry. I was just messing with you," he said as he continued to chuckle.

"I don't see anything funny!

"I'm sorry I was just thinking about what you said about if we ran into each other a third time. Well, this is the third time," he said with a big smile showing those sexy dimples.

"No, actually this is the fourth time, I saw you with your wife Nicole about a week ago in the waiting room, when your friend was shot," I stated frankly.

"Third or fourth time, doesn't matter. It's always a pleasure to see a beautiful face!"

"Please don't go there. I have had my share of married men. If you were single, then we could talk, but I learned my lesson with marriage men and I'm done. Goodbye, Brian," I said and walked off.

"Rachel! Wait!" He said as he caught up to me. "How are your boys doing?"

When he asked me that question, my knees got so weak that I almost fell. He grabbed my arm and caught me and told me to sit down for a while. For a brief second, our eyes met and I could tell that he was genuinely concerned and I'm sure he saw the sadness in my eyes. When we sat down I told him about my boys.

"Aww, Rachel! I'm so sorry. I'll be praying for your family," he said to me.

"How is your friend?" I asked him.

"Oh, he is doing well. He is preparing to be released in a few days. Be strong, Rachel. God has the final say and whatever is his will, it shall be done, but just remember God will never give us more than we can bear he helps us carry our burdens if we would just ask. Have a great day, Rachel," Brian said to me and walked away.

I headed to the family room and laid across the bed and before I even realized it, I was asleep. I had a dream that seemed so real that I woke up in tears.

It took me a minute to realize where I was, but as I looked around I saw I was still in the hospital family room. The dream was not true!

I had a dream that Mikye and Mikele was about three years old and they were both dressed in all white. I had on a white flowing sundress and we were all running in this field that was filled with sunflowers and daisies. When we all got tired of running, we laid on this big red blanket on the ground and the twins started talking to me.

Mikye was talking about angels. He said he saw two angels playing in the clouds. He kept pointing to the sky trying to make me see them, but I didn't see anything. Then he said, "Mommy, I want to be an angel, so I can play in the clouds." I remember saying to him, "No baby, you can't be an angel right now because Mommy will miss you." He looked at me and said, "But mommy, I'll always be with you. I'll be your angel," and he just smiled at me.

Mikele came over to me and sat on my lap. He gave me a big hug and kiss and said, "Mommy, God wants us to be his angels, so we have to go. I'll watch out for Mikye, I promise."

I squeezed Mikele tighter to me and told him, "No baby, you can't leave me. You just can't." I remember reaching out to Mikye and he walked over and hugged me and Mikele and as I held them, they started to disappear. After a while, Mikye and Mikele was flying, holding hands, into this big, fluffy cloud. They both looked back at me and said, "Mommy, we love you and we will always watch over you!"

My eyes filled with tears and reached out for my boys, but they started to disappear. I woke up sweating and with tears running down my face.

9
DEREK

Leaving home this time was hard because I knew that Persia and I would never be together again.

I should have told her about Taylor. I should have told her everything so we could start anew, but I hid my affair with Taylor.

Good thing, I hadn't move my things back in with Persia and I still had my room at the hotel for the week.

The ride back to the hotel was one of self-reflection. Everything I had done wrong to Persia, Keshia, and even Taylor were haunting me. All of my bad decisions had come back to bit me in the ass and I can't blame anyone but myself. I was the selfish one. I wanted things my way and I didn't care who I hurt.

After all the dirt to the people in my life, the only one that ended up dirty was me! Keshia was moving on with her life and Desiree was getting to know her father, Antwan. Desiree used to call and text me, but now I rarely hear from her. The look in Persia's eyes and how calm she was with Taylor, let's me know that she is really done this time.

Part of me wanted to scold Taylor for what she did, but another part of me missed her. Not only were we lovers, but we were friends. I could talk to Taylor about anything and right now I could really use a friend. I'll be back on the road in a few days and the time alone will be wonderful for me to sort things out and decide what I'm going to do to fix the craziness in my life.

Instead of going straight to the room, I decided to go to strip club. I figure looking at ass and titties while drinking would calm my nerves or at least stop me from thinking about the fucked up situation that just happened.

I made it to the club just in time for the midnight show. *Stilettos* was known for having super sexy, super thick dancers, and the midnight show was always the best. When I arrived at the club, the deejay was announcing a dancer named Kandi to the stage. She was dancing to *Lollipop* by Lil' Wayne.

I've never seen this dancer at the club before but her ass was hypnotizing. The men flocked to the stage, throwing cash her way. Even some women were standing at the stage enjoying the show. If I was able to get closer to the stage, I definitely would have gotten a closer look as well.

By the time the song ended, the stage was covered in money. Two of the bouncers came out and help Kandi gather her money.

I sat down at the bar and order some *Patron* shots will watching the dancers come and go off the stage. After an hour or so, I saw Kandi emerge from the back and started giving lap dances. I watched her from afar wishing that I had sat at one of the tables, so she could dance for me. Most of the tables were filled, so I just continued sitting at the bar.

I may have went overboard with the shots because I was too tipsy to drive. I was probably one or two shots away from the bartender shutting me down for the night. I had to call someone to come get me because there was no way I was going to leave my car in this area overnight.

The only person, I could call was Taylor and even though I was still kind of pissed at her from what she did, I really needed her to come through for me.

I called Taylor and after about five rings, she finally answered the phone.

"Taylor, this is Derek. I need you to catch a cab to Stilettos and come get me. I drove my car to the club, because I'm too tipsy to drive."

"Derek, why would you get drunk, knowing you had to drive?" she said sleepily.

"I don't need your lectures after the stunt you just pulled tonight. So you coming or not?"

"I'm coming, just hang tight," she said with a slight attitude and hung up before I could respond.

After almost an hour, Taylor showed up and we left the club.

"So, where are we going?" She inquired.

"Ummm" is the last thing I remember but I was out like a light.

When I woke up, it was almost morning, I reached over and felt someone in the bed with me. I sat up straight and realized that it was Taylor. After my eyes adjusted to the room, I realized we were not in my hotel room.

I didn't want to wake Taylor, but I had to piss like hell. I eased out the bed and went to the bathroom. When I got back to the bed, Taylor were stirring in her sleep, but she didn't wake up. I climbed back into bed, kissed Taylor on her neck and drifted off to sleep.

I awoke to small kisses on my neck and the side of my face, the smell of food, a blinding headaches, and a growling stomach.

"Go wash up and come eat. I picked up some *Waffle House* and aspirins. Hopefully the sausage will help settle your stomach."

"Okay," I said trying to adjust my eyes to the light in the room.

After I washed up, we ate breakfast in silence. Taylor looked like she had a lot to say, but she didn't know how to say it. Considering the fact that my head was still hurting, I didn't push to find out what she wanted to say to me.

I guess she realized that I wasn't going to ask her what was wrong and she finally spoke up.

"Derek, I'm sorry!" I know you probably still mad at me, and you should be. I never should have come to your home like that," she said with tears in her eyes.

"Taylor, it's okay! What's done is done! Plus that relationship was broken long before you knocked on that door."

"Okay," she muttered while wiping the tears that managed to escape her eyes. Then she got up and went into the bathroom.

I finished eating and Taylor was still in the bathroom. I got up to see if she was alright.

"Taylor, are you okay in there?

She didn't answer me, but I heard her sniffing and water start to run. I turned the knob and entered the bathroom. Taylor was the sink splashing water on her face. I stood behind her and wrapped my arms around her. I'm not sure why I did that but surprisingly it felt good.

I can't remember the last time I had genuine affection and intimacy for and from anyone. Lately, it's all been about sex, even with Persia we were just always going through the motions. Somehow, Taylor always seems to connect with me, not only physically but emotionally and being around her like this after so much time apart was igniting a fire in me that only Taylor could put out.

She turned around in my arms and I saw she still had tears in eyes. I wiped her tears and we kissed. I missed feeling her. I missed being with her. I missed everything about her. Now that I had her in my grasp, I wasn't ready to just let her go.

We got naked in record time, and I picked up Taylor and carried her to the bed. I didn't just want sex from Taylor; I wanted to make love to her. I kissed her from her forehead to her cheeks, stopping to make love to her ears with a few deep kisses on the lips in between, while I made my way down to her neck and eventually her chest.

Her perky breasts called out to me and my lips answered. I licked around her nipples, teasing her until she grabbed my head and shoved it to her favorite breast. With each lick or kiss, I could feel Taylor relinquishing all of her power to me and fully submitting to me. I went from breast to breast equally making love to them with mouth.

Once Taylor started squirming, I guided my hands between her legs and found her opening and pushed my fingers inside of her. Then I kissed from her breasts down to her navel and back up again until I was harassing her breasts with my lips.

Taylor couldn't take it anymore and begged me to stop. After I realized, she really wanted me to stop, I seized pleasuring her and laid back on the bed. She straddled me and started kissing on me from my forehead to my chest like I did her.

She wasted no time putting me in her mouth. She always could suck my dick the best and tonight she was putting in extra work, since we haven't been together in a long time. I felt my dick hit the back of her throat as my love juice slide down her throat. I thought that she would stop, but instead that made her go harder. She sucked me from soft back to hard again. Once I was rock hard, she removed me from her and mouth and said, "Make love to me!"

She didn't have to ask me, that exactly what I was planning to do.

10

BRIAN

Seeing Nicole in that white negligee was turning me on so bad. I wanted to fuck her right there on the living room floor, but she insisted on eating dinner first. Dinner looked delicious, but my mind was on her.

Do you know how it feel so want something to bad and have to wait for it? I can't remember the last time Nicole and I made love and the fact that she was willing to give me some, but make me wait for it was pure torture.

Halfway through dinner, I couldn't take it anymore. I got up, pulled her chair from the table, got on my knees and started kissing her, while removing her underwear at the same time. I thought she would stop me, but she didn't. I think my aggressiveness were turning her on, because she lifted up out of the chair, so I could remove her thongs.

After I had her underwear taken off, I dove right in and she was sweeter than a Georgia peach. To get better access to my dessert, I lifted her right leg over the arm of the chair and pull her body down towards me, closer to my mouth. I planted small kisses on the inside of her thighs and back up to her hot, throbbing pussy before covering it with my mouth, while making figure eights with my tongue up and down, going deeper and deeper with each lick. Right before she was about to explode, I stopped picked her up and carried her to our bedroom.

I wanted to make love to her slowly, softly, and sensual, but the urge to simply fuck her overtook me and the image of her on all four, while I drilled my dick in and out her became overbearing.

I turned Nicole onto her stomach. "Head down, ass up!" I told her. She did as I asked while her ass fell open line a broken heart. My dick got rock hard, just from watching her perfectly round ass with tiny dimples and the little mole on her left cheek.

I ran my hand from the top of her ass all the way down to her pussy. She was so wet that my fingers slipped inside of her. I pushed my fingers in and out of while planting kisses on her lower back. I removed my fingers and thrusted my dick inside her.

Once she identified my rhythm, she matched it. Even if I slowed down or sped up, Nicole still match my rhythm. When I felt my body about to explode, I slowed down and pulled out for a moment. When I was ready to start again, Nicole wouldn't let me put all of my dick inside of her, instead she rode the head. She started out slow, almost teasing me then she started going faster and faster until I burst inside of her.

I pulled out and she turned onto her back and started fingering her pussy until she was squirting all over the bed. Watching her play with herself was turning me on.

I was having so much fun watching her play with herself that I went into the bathroom closet and removed her sex toy box off the top shelf. I took out her massager from *Bedroom Kandi* and teased her with the massager.

The way her body moved effortless with the massager let me know that she was used to pleasuring herself. She can be a freak whenever she wants to. Most times, I don't get to see the dark side of my wife, but tonight she has really exposed her inner freak.

I know she has a freaky side, though. She has been trying to get me to have a threesome for months, but I won't do it. I just feel like once we open the door; it's going to be hard to close, especially since Nicole is attracted to women. She think I don't know, but I notice how she checks out women, when we are together and she thinks I'm not looking.

A threesome would be a lot of fun, I'm sure. What man wouldn't want to have two women pleasing him and themselves at the same time? Watching that movie *Trios'* will have anybody caution of a threesome, that shit can backfire.

Refocusing my attention to Nicole, I see her body start to convulse, and as if on cue, my dick got rock hard. I joined her on the bed and replaced her massager with the real thing. Every time I thrusted my dick into her, she lift up off the bed just a little to match my stroke. We continued with the grinding tug of war until both of our body started seizing and once again I filled her up with my love juice. Then we both just stretched out on the bed, catching our breads.

I don't know what she was thinking about but I was thinking about kids. Tonight was the first time in a long time that Nicole let me have sex with her without using protection or pulling out. I pray one of my soldiers find an egg and attach to it as soon as possible.

As I start to drift off to sleep, I reach over and hug Nicole and brought her closer to me and before long, we both were fast asleep.

11

RACHEL

I wiped the tears that was coming from my eyes and I woke up. After finally getting myself together, I threw on my shoes and ran back down to the NICU.

"Are my babies ok?" I screamed at the nurse at the front desk. She looked at me as if I was crazy. Mikye and Mikele Dawson, are they okay? Again she looked at me as if I was crazy. I tried to calm down and speak slower and more rational.

"Nurse, I'm sorry. I've just woke up and I want to know if everything is okay with my boys that's all. I can't wait until visitation. Can you please just call and see how my babies are doing?"

"Sure ma'am. Give me just a minute," she said to me.

So many thoughts played in my head and time seemed to be at a standstill. The nurse finally got off the phone and said that a doctor was coming out to speak to me.

"Thank you ma'am and I'm so sorry for my behavior," I said sorrowfully.

"It's okay, I completely understand," she said.

After what seemed like ten or fifteen minutes the doctor came out and got me and told me to follow him to the family conference room. My knees got weak and I couldn't move. The doctor seeing the shock and worry on my face, helped me up and walked me to the room.

Once we got to the room, the doctor told me it would be best if I called, Mr. Dawson and any other family I wanted to be there with me. He told me, he would give me a few moments to do that and he would be back.

With my hands shaking, I dialed Mike's number. Each unanswered ring made my heart stop and start again. Finally he answered on the fourth ring.

"Get to the hospital, ASAP!" I said to him.

"What? What's going on Rachel?" he asked.

"Mike just get here, now!" I said and hung up the phone.

I called my mom and told her to come to the hospital and bring my other children.

After a torturous hour or so, everyone was at the hospital and packed into the conference room. Dr. Robinson entered the room and everyone got quiet. Mike sat beside me and when he saw Dr. Robinson, he grabbed my hand under the table and squeezed it tight. I was so nervous, and I could tell that he was nervous, too.

"Hello, everyone. I know you all are wondering why I called you all here today, but I wanted to give you an update on the boys. As you all know the boys were initially diagnosed with a bacterial infection called *cronobacter sakazakii*. We finally found an antibiotic to counteract the infection, however the infection has spread and become a form of meningitis, called *septicemia*. If the infection reaches the blood, it is highly problematic for infants. Since the twins aren't old enough to be vaccinated, and their bodies are too small for advanced antibiotics treatment. So for safety measures, we have the boys in a medically-induced coma to stop the infection from spreading any further and to protect the twins against seizures," Dr. Robinson said.

Sniffling could be heard throughout the room. Mike squeezed my hand harder and tighter under the table. He was trying hard not to let the tears that filled his eyes fall but they still escaped. I let my tears run freely. I had lost all energy to even wipe them away.

Dr. Robinson continued, "I know this is hard to hear, but I have to prepare for what may be coming. The twins are not responding to the medication as they should and at this stage, things can get better or significantly worse. Just know we are doing the absolute best we can considering the circumstances. Do anyone have any questions for me?"

Nobody said anything at first, Mike and I looked at each other and I knew he wanted to say something. I wanted to say it too, but we were both afraid saying it out loud would make it come true. I didn't tell Mike about the dream I had. I didn't tell anyone. I was afraid to say anything about it, but now my dream and Dr. Robinson update on my boys were analogous.

I had to ask. I don't think I am strong enough to hear the answer, but I have to know. "Doctor, in your professional opinion, are my babies going to make it?" More sniffles could be heard throughout the room.

Dr. Robinson thought for a minute before saying, "In severe meningitis cases like this, we have seen patients get better, but those patients were not infants. We have seen some patient overcome meningitis with little to moderate brain damage. Our greatest challenge with the boys, is that they are too young for the vaccination and their bodies are too small and too weak for stronger antibiotics. All I can tell you is that we are doing the absolute best we can to save those babies.

Tears were falling from ever eye in the room, except the doctor. "Thank you, Dr. Robinson, I appreciate your honesty," I said.

As soon as I said that, Dr. Robinson's pager started going off and he was called over the loud speaker.

"I will give you an update later and thanks for beings so patient and understanding. Just take a seat back out in the waiting area until the next visiting hour," Dr. Robinson said and hurriedly left the room.

I felt a strong pain in my chest once Dr. Robinson walked out that door. I can't explain the pain or the feeling, but I had to get to the boys. I felt like they needed me, like they needed their mom.

"I'll be right back," I whispered to Mike. As I walked down the hallway and turned the corner to my boys' room, I saw nurses running in and out of the room. Before I could even register what was happening, the tears started and almost blinded me as I ran to the room to see what was going on.

Two nurses restrained me before I could see exactly what was going on, but I saw them working on Mikye.

I tried to break past the two nurses that were holding me back, but I couldn't.

"What's happening with Mikye? What are they doing? Why can't I see him? Please tell me what is going on with my son! Please!" I was asking a million questions, but I wasn't getting a straight answer.

"Ma'am, please come down, we are doing the best we can right now, but I need you to calm down and let us do our jobs.

Mike came down the hall and I ran into his arms, trying to tell what was going on through my muffled tears.

"What's wrong, Rachel? What's going on?" He asked me confused yet concerned. I pulled away from Mike's embrace.

"Some-something's wrong with Mikye, but they won't tell me what's wrong!"

Mike eyes got bigger as he started questioning the nurses. The nurses were about to respond when we saw Dr. Robinson and two other nurses exit the room with their heads down. One of the nurses were crying really hard.

I wanted to run to the room to check on my babies, but I couldn't move. I couldn't talk. I couldn't do anything. Temporary paralysis had taken over my body and although I could see everything going on around me, I couldn't react.

When I was finally able to move, I started to walk towards the twins' room, and everything went black.

12

TAMMIE

It's been over a week since the incident in the hospital. I can't believe that I allowed Mike and Rachel to make me act like a fool in that hospital. Fighting in a chapel and for what? A husband that has already had one foot out the door for the last few months.

I realize now that I would never have 100% of Mike anymore. Rachel isn't going anywhere. Rachel is Mike's addiction. He just can't let her go, so I decided to stop playing games and give him the one thing he wants—to be free!

I have to meet with Mrs. Templeton, the family lawyer that worked on Persia's case, later to work up my divorce papers and get them sent to Mike as soon as possible. I haven't heard from him since the fight at the hospital. Of course the kids were asking about him, but I just told them that Daddy was busy working out of town. I hated lying to my kids, but I really didn't know what else to tell them. Mike has not call them or came around since the twins been in the hospital. I don't even know where he has been staying.

I had a few hours before my meeting with my lawyer. I texted Persia and Sharon told her to meet me for drinks a little later. We haven't hung out together in a long time. Normally, I would have told them everything that's been going on and have them with me for support, but this time, I just realize that this is something I must do alone.

To kill time until my meeting with the lawyer, I decided to go shopping. Retail therapy is always helpful and it's also the perfect place for eye candy. Not that I was looking, but it would be nice to see some eye candy and possibly window shop in that department for future use.

Today didn't disappoint, the mall was filled with big sales and fine guys. There were fine black guys, white guys, Hispanic guys, guys with dreads, bald heads, Mohawks, low fades, etc. You name it, I probably saw it. A few guys tried to get my attention, but I wasn't interested. They just didn't seem like my type.

I was in footlocker trying on shoes when someone called my name.

"Tammie Dawson!"

I stopped trying on the shoe and looked up and it was JAMAL! Despite what happened between us, he was still fine as hell. He had on a white oxford shirt with fitted dark blue jeans and casual like shoes.

Flashbacks of what happened between us the last time we were together played in my head. I was speechless. I didn't know whether to scream or to run! Jamal must have seen the worry in my eyes.

"Tammie, I'm not going to hurt you," he said with sincerity.

"Hello, Jamal," I said nervously.

"Tammie, can I talk to you? I just want the chance to formally apologize for hurting you the way I did. Just hear me out and I promise that I won't bother you again."

"Okay, Jamal. We can talk at the food court."

We left out the shoe store and sat down at the food court.

"Tammie, it's crazy how things work out. I was going to try to contact you, but look at how fate works. Anyway, I want you to know that I've been in therapy since the incident between us and I went to rehab for my addiction. I've been clean ever since that day and I also finally learned to deal with the one thing I was running from. I never told you about my daughter Brianna's death or the real reason my wife, Tameka and I divorced. My wife killed my daughter. She left her in a hot car all day and forgot about her. I came home and found my daughter dead, still strapped in her car seat. That was the worse day of my life. I lost my daughter and I gained an undeniable hatred for my wife. My wife became severely depressed, tried to kill herself, and ended up being hospitalized. I couldn't look at her without thinking of what she did, so we divorced."

"Oh, Jamal. I'm so sorry! I didn't know!"

"For years, I secretly dealt with the pain of losing my daughter and because of it I ran from any form of a relationship. I was afraid that as soon as I get happy again, it would be taken from me, again. The day of the incident between us was the anniversary of my daughter's death. I'm not making excuses for what I did because I was wrong, dead wrong for what I did to you. But when I realized that you were trying to end things with me I snapped. You were the first woman I loved after my wife and to have you walk away from just got to me. I hope that you can forgive me. Like I said, I've been in therapy since then dealing with my feelings and I still attend meetings for my addiction, even though I would only relapse on that day. But now instead of getting high and trying to block out the pain of the day of my daughter's death, I've learned to embrace it and celebrate the time she was here instead of focusing on her death. We are working on making amends in therapy and I really want to apology to you for everything I did to you"

"That's wonderful, Jamal! I'm happy for you. I forgive you. I have a meeting soon, but it was nice talking to you."

"One more thing before you leave, How are you doing, Tammie? You seem like something is bothering you."

"How would you know when something is bothering me, Jamal?"

"Believe it or not Tammie, the little time we did share together, I actually paid attention to you and I could always tell when something was bothering you and contrary to what you think, everything I felt for you was real!"

"Okay, Jamal but I really have to get going. It was nice seeing you again."

"It was nice seeing you too!"

I met with Mrs. Templeton, got my divorce papers worked up and arranged for her to serve Mike at his job. Since the meeting didn't last long and Sharon was about to get off work, I called Persia and arranged for her to meet Sharon and I earlier than we planned at the Red Lobster off East-West Connector.

*****

Sharon and I arrived at the restaurant a few minutes before Persia got there. We ordered drinks and appetizers and made small talk until Persia arrived.

It's been a while since we all hung out together like we used to do for our weekly lunches, except this time, our lives were in shamble. Sharon informed us of the situation with her and Nicole. Persis informed us of Derek and Taylor, and I gave them an update on the situation between Mike and me.

Persia and Sharon avoided bringing up the topic of Rachel and Mike. I guess they didn't know how I would take it.

"Have you guys heard from Rachel or Mike lately? He hasn't been home. He doesn't answer any of my calls or texts. He's still mad at me for what I did in Hawaii."

"I haven't talked to either of them in a few days," Persia stated.

"I haven't either. I had to go back to work and Rachel isn't answering her phone or texts," Sharon state.

The waitress came and took our orders and we talked a little bit more about the issues going on in each other's lives but then we started talking about other things like work, kids, favorite T.V. shows, etc.

My mind fell on Jamal. I didn't tell Persia and Sharon about meeting with Jamal because I knew they would over react.

We ate in silenced. It was weird. We used to have so much to talk about when we were did our weekly lunch now nobody knew what to say. We were all riding the thin line because we didn't want to risk saying something that would hurt someone feelings.

Even though, we didn't talk as much as usual, it still felt great to be around my friends again. We finished up our dinner, made plans to link up later in the week, and went our separate ways.

Driving home, I couldn't stop thinking about Mike. I could stop thinking about how happy, we used to be. Despite all that Mike and I are going through, I have to admit that I really do miss him, but I'm not going to continue to compete with Rachel. I shouldn't have to but the fact that he hasn't been home says that he has made his decision.

I thought finally filing the papers would make me happy or make me feel good, but it did the opposite. Filing the papers made me sad and slightly angry. This isn't the way I planned for my marriage to end. I thought maybe we could find a way to make our marriage work, but I guess not. I rather be alone than to continue a marriage with someone that is always cheating on me.

13

PERSIA

It was nice catching up with Tammie and Sharon. It didn't feel like the old days, but it was great being together again. With everything that's going on, it's been really hard for us to get together.

We all been having relationship issues and it is nice having people around that understand what you are going through. As for my situation, I'm done with Derek. Taylor was the final straw. Maybe we could have worked through our issues, if he had been upfront about Taylor after I found out about Keisha.

I know I'm not perfect and I've done my share of dirt, but Deniji and Antwan are the only two men I was with besides my husband and he knew about them both. Taylor, messy ass, showing up on my door steps was the last straw. Maybe I could have respected her more if she had approached me like a woman and not like a teenage girl staking claim on a man that didn't belong to either of us. I guess she will finally get what she wanted---DEREK!

My kids are staying with my sister tonight, and I didn't feel like going home to an empty house. I texted Deniji to see if he wanted to chill for a while.

We still talked occasionally but we haven't been intimate since the day, we did the threesome.

I felt a little guilty about being with Antwan and Deniji at the same time, but I don't regret it. I wanted that experience, so I did it. I only felt bad because Antwan got his feelings involved. I guess, he really liked me. I had no clue, he felt that way. We've always been good friends with benefits, so it was hard for me to see that he wanted a relationship. We are back to being friends, but this time we are simply friends. Antwan and Keisha are dating and he is enjoying being a father.

I didn't want to go home after catching up with Tammie and Sharon. I decided to kick it with Deniji, but I had to figure out where. My house would only make me think of Derek and I didn't want to go to his apartment because then I would be worried about his girlfriend popping up. So, I just texted him.

Me: Hey! How are you doing? I'm out and about, want to join me?

Deniji: Hey stranger! Surprised you want to see me, you restricted me to text and calls only. I actually been meaning to talk to you about something anyway? Come over.

Me: You sure that's a good idea. What about your little girlfriend?

Deniji: Why would I invite you over, if she was here? Just come over. Okay?

Me: Okay.

I arrived at Deniji's apartment and he answered the door with no shirt on. He still had an awesome body and it still was hypnotizing to me. His smooth, chocolate skin, tight abs were screaming for my lips to kiss them and my hands to rub them. Before I could do anything, he grabbed me and kissed me long, hard, and deep. We kissed so long I had to pull away.

"I see I was missed!"

"Yes, you were now shut up and kiss me again!" Deniji commanded.

I didn't argue with him. I did as I was told and relished the sweetness of his tongue as it explored the inside my mouth. With every kiss, I was getting more and more turned on. I started to take my clothes off and Deniji stopped me, took my hand and led me to the sofa.

"I want to talk to you about something," he said sternly while putting on a shirt.

"Okay, I'm listening," I said while secretly wishing he had kept his shirt off.

"Well, this is not easy for me to say, but I have to say it. I know you only see me as your little boy toy or bust it baby, but Persia, I want more. I want to be so much more. I know I'm young, but I know you feeling me. I see the way you look at me. I feel it when we kiss. I see your smile, whenever we text and your heart screams out to me when we have sex. The last time we were together was amazing. I felt your heart connect with mines and I know you felt it to. It started out as sex but it turned into something more. We were so into each other and for a moment you took down your barriers and let me in. I see how hard you try not to look into my eyes, but that day, you looked in my eyes and kissed me with so much passion. What I'm trying to say is you don't have to act so hard with me. I feel what you feel and I want to be with you, Persia."

"Deniji, I don't know what to say to that. I'm sorry. I think I better go."

"There you go running again. For you to be a strong-willed woman, you are so scary. You run from the things that makes you happy. When we first started this, I know it was only a sex thing. It was cool with you using me because never in my life have being used felt so good, but then things start to evolve, or so I thought and I thought we were getting closer. I was wrong. I must have misread all those signs that I thought told me you had feelings for me as well. I'm sorry, Persia. I shouldn't have assumed about anything. If you want to go, go ahead. Lock the door on your way out!" Deniji said and went to his bedroom and closed the door, leaving me on the sofa dumbfounded.

I started to go back and talk to him but I didn't. I had already hurt his feelings there was no point in rubbing salt in the wound. The truth is I do like Deniji, but right now at this point in my life, I want to be alone. I want to spend some time getting myself together first before jumping into another relationship.

I gathered my things and left, locking his door behind me as he directed. As I reached my car door, I heard his front door open and he was headed towards me. When he reached me, he pinned me again the car and kissed me deeper than I've ever been kissed. I kissed him back with just as much passion as he kissed me. He broke the kiss and said to me, "I love you, Persia!" Then he turned around and left me standing at my car.

Although these little temper tantrums of his were childish and pissing me off, in a weird, sort of way they were turning me on like hell. *Why are Nigerian men so stubborn?*

I couldn't leave with Deniji thinking I didn't feel the same. I didn't want to leave horny either. I don't know which reason was stronger in getting me to go back inside the house, but I went. I entered the house again and locked the door. By the time I got to Deniji's bedroom there was a trail of my clothes from the door to his room.

He was laying across the bed with his hand behind his head and looking as if he was in deep thought. When he saw that I was naked, he started to get up.

"Stay right there. Just like that," I commanded him.

I walked over to the bed and straddled him. I kissed him long, hard, and deep just like he had kissed me earlier. I could feel his dick rising under me as our tongues continued to wrestle. I broke our kiss and started kissing up and down his body. From his lips to his ears to his neck and chest before eventually making my way to his rigid magic stick. I hungrily put his dick in my mouth and began sucking him until he hit the back of my throat. Then, I started going up and down on his dick with my mouth. His body started to convulse and I knew he was about to cum, so I slowed down and pulled his dick out of my mouth until only the tip remained and I sucked on the tip of his dick like I was sucking on a popsicle on a hot, summer day and just like a popsicle melts in your mouth, Deniji melted all in my mouth and down my throat and I savored every last drop.

When I finally sat up, Deniji was still frozen in place. I don't know if he was in shock or still in deep thought.

"Are you okay?" I asked.

"Yea, yea. I'm good, actually, I'm great! Damn girl you making me fall in love with you for real!" He said.

His strong African accent turning me on at every vowel he spoke.

"Okay, well how bout you show me how much you love me? You know actions speak louder than words!" I said teasing Deniji.

Deniji sat up on the edge of the bed.

"Come here!"

I did as I was told. He outlined my body with his hands before guided his hand to my hot honey pot and inserting two fingers inside of me. For a moment, his fingers danced inside of me.

Looking down at Deniji, I could no longer deny looking into his eyes. I could see that this man loved me. I could see that he truly cared for me. This was more than sex to him. The small beams of lights breaking through his blinds were highlighting his gorgeous dark skin in the sexiest way.

I don't know if what I was feeling was love, lust, or loneliness. All I know is that at this moment this was where I wanted to be.

Deniji stood up, picked me up, and carried me to the nearest wall. With my back against the wall, he squatted until his face was between my legs. I don't know how he managed to hold me against the wall, while he ate my honey, but I enjoyed every single moment. Just as my body was about to go into convulsions, he stopped and gently put me down.

"Bend over and touch your toes!" he demanded.

"I don't think I can touch my toes," I said.

"Go as far as you can."

Once again, I did as I was told and without warning, Deniji thrusted his dick into me. I didn't take long before I was creaming all over his dick, but he still didn't stop. Once I found his rhythm, I matched it. Whenever he grinded inward, I twerked out. I bounced my ass onto his dick. After a while, both our bodies were convulsing. After catching our breath, we collapsed onto the bed. I don't know who fell asleep first, but I awoke the next morning in his arms.

I could get used to waking up to him every morning, but for now, I'll just enjoy today because I have no idea what tomorrow will bring for Deniji and I.

14

RACHEL

I woke up in a hospital bed. Even though, I was still a little groggy. I could tell that Mike had been crying.

"Wh-what happened, Mike? Why am I in a hospital bed?" Before Mike could answer Dr. Robinson and a nurse came in and Mike came around to the other side of the bed.

Tears was now flooding from Mike's eyes. I could tell something was wrong. Even without the details my tears started filling up my eyes. Mike grabbed my hand. I looked up at the doctor and part of me knew what he wanted to say, but I still needed to hear it. Before I blacked out, I remember the doctor coming out the twins' room. That's all I can remember.

"Ms. Williams, I'm sorry but Mikye passed away at 11:48 a.m. this morning. The infection spread to his brain and he had a seizure in his sleep."

I looked up at the clock and it was almost four in the evening. I heard what the doctor said, but the words were not registering in my mind. I felt the tears running down my face but I couldn't talk.

"Ms. Williams, did you hear what I just said to you?" Dr. Robinson asked me with concern in his voice.

I shook my head yes. Dr. Robinson, pulled out his microscopic light and started looking in my eyes calling my name.

"I'm okay, Doctor. Can I see my boys now?"

Dr. Robinson looked from me to Mike as if he was asking Mike's permission.

"I want to see my children. Now, Doctor!" I yelled at him.

"Ms. Williams, are you understanding what I said about Mikye? Ms. Williams? Ms. Williams, Mikye is dead! Mikele is still holding on. He is stable for now, but we have noticed some changes in his condition that is threatening his recovery."

"I understand, Doctor. Thank you. I know you tried your best. Can I see him, now?"

Again, the doctor looked at Mike.

"Can you please stop looking at Mike every time I ask you a question? He is not my father nor is he my husband. He is just my children's father. Now again, can I see my son?"

I got up out the bed and started putting on my shoes. The tears in my eyes were falling, but I couldn't bring myself to cry out, even though on the inside I was dying a slow death. My chest tighten like I was having a heart attack and my breathing sped up so much so that I thought I was going to pass back out or have a panic attack.

"Mrs. Williams, are you okay? Are you sure you up to this right now? Maybe you should rest a little bit more?"

"No, Doctor. I'm okay. I just want to see my baby!"

"Ms. Williams, the nurse will take you to the morgue to see Baby Mikye. Baby Mikele is still in critical condition, just let the nurse know when you ready to see him and she will take you to see him as well. I'm sorry for your lost, Ms. Williams," the doctor said and left the room.

"Do you want me to go with you, Rachel?" Mike asked.

"No, I'm okay. Just go check on Mikele. Make sure he is doing okay!"

I followed the nurse to the morgue and she informed the nurse at the window who we were there to see. The nurse pulled out one of the drawers, pulled back the white sheet, and left.

"I'll be right outside the door. If you need me, let me know," said the nurse that I came with. Once the door closed behind the nurse, I slowly walked over to where my son's lifeless body laid. He looked as if he was just sleeping. I reached out and touched his hand and it was cold. I held his hand up to my lips and kiss his little hands as tears ran down my face. I put his hand back at his side and kiss him on the forehead. I wanted to hold him one last time, but I was afraid of bruising his body or something. I kissed Mikye on his cheeks as I whispered in his ear.

"I love you, baby! I'll always love you. Guess you can play in the clouds now!" I said as I remembered the dream I had. As much as I wanted my son here with me, God had other plans and he had already shown me that my son would be okay.

I pulled the sheet back over my son's face and pushed the drawer closed. In my dream, Mikele was also an angel, so if my dream was coming true, then Mikele's time was drawing to an end as well. I begin to panic.

"I want to see Mikele, now!" I screamed at the nurse.

The elevator ride back to the NICU was extremely quiet and seemed to take forever. I prayed so many prayers in the span of that short elevator ride that I'm not even sure God himself heard them all. The nurse wanted to say something to comfort me, but I could tell she didn't know what to say. What do you say to comfort a grieving mother? I'm not even sure that there is anything that anyone could say to a grieving mother that would comfort her.

I was dying on the inside and the tears were falling on the outside. I felt numb and lost. I wanted to blame God, Tammie, Mike, or anyone else that I could think of and hope that it would make me feel better, but I know that it won't.

When I reached the room, Mike was there sitting by Mikele's bed. He appeared to be praying or he had dozed off to sleep.

I hurried passed the bed where Mikye had been while resisting the urge to breakdown and cry. All the linen had been removed from the bed and the machines had been removed. Tears filled my eyes, but I tried my best to stop them from falling.

I walked up behind Mike and tapped him on the shoulder and that's when I saw that he had been crying, also.

His eyes were blood shot red and some of his tears still stained his face. He started to say something to me, but instead he grabbed me by my waist and just hugged me really tight. My tears escaped my eyes and cascaded down my face.

Because he was sitting down, his head fell just below my breasts, I rubbed one of my hands through his hair, while patting him on the back with the other one.

I wanted to comfort him and tell him everything would be okay, but I wasn't sure if I really believed that. I lost one son and I still had one barely holding on.

The dream I had about Mikele and Mikye kept playing in my head. I still haven't told Mike or anyone else about the dream I had.

We hugged in silence for about five minutes before Mike released me. I walked over to the other side of the bed and stroked Mikele's hand, while Mike held his other one.

"I love you, Mikele! Always remember, momma loves you!" I whispered in his ear and kissed him on the jaw.

When I kissed him, I was overcome with an eerie feeling. A chill went through my body and the hairs on my hands and the back of my neck stood up. I gazed at Mikele and his cheeks seemed pale.

Visions from my dream flashed through my head and again I started to panic.

"Mike? Something's wrong with Mikele, I can feel it!" I said. I pushed the button to call the nurse and ask her to come right away. The nurse came in and asked us to give her some space so she could examine Mikele. As she checked the machines and did a quick examination of him, her demeanor appeared to change.

"I'm going to have the doctor come in and do a thorough examination of Mikele," the nurse said.

I heard the uncertainty in her voice and I knew something was wrong.

The nurse left to go get the doctor and I scurried back to Mikele's bedside. I stroked his face and whispered in his ear again that I loved him. I peeped up at the machines and I saw his heart rate fluctuate up and down.

"Take care of Mikye. He'll be waiting for you," I murmured in his ear and kissed him on the cheek once more. This time his skin was cool to the touch.

I don't know why I felt so calm saying that to Mikele, even though the pain of possibly losing both of my babies were wearing me down like quicksand. I walked away from the side of the bed I was on to the side where Mike stood. He was struggling to keep the tears from falling down his face.

He bent down and kissed Mikele's cheek as well and turned to leave, but stopped once he saw Dr. Robinson enter.

"Spotting Mike's nervousness, Dr. Robinson said, "I just want to examine him to see if there has been any changes."

Mike and I watched Dr. Robinson examined Mikele and just like the nurse, his demeanor change. He had a dire look on his face.

Mike walked next to me and good thing he did, because my knees were getting weak from the nervousness.

"What is it doctor?" Mike spoke up.
"I'll know more once I get another CATscan done. Because we can't move him, they will come here to do the scan. The nurse already called radiology and they should be up soon. I truly appreciated your patience with me during this difficult time and my condolences to your family. You guys are welcome to stay until the x-ray techs get here, but then you need to wait in the family conference rooms," the doctor said and left the room.

Mike and I both cried and prayed over Mikele. After a few minutes, the techs arrived and we left and went to the conference room. Mike was pacing back and forth, eyes redder than a fireball.

"Sit down, Mike! Get some rest!" I pleaded.

Mike finally sat down and put his head down on the table. I moved closer to him and rubbed his back. That simple act made him break down. I have never seen Mike so emotional. Seeing him so distraught, made me hysterical and before long we were both crying our eyes out, while trying to comfort each other and plea to God to please save our child.

God must had other plans, because after another thirty minutes in the conference room, the doctor came in and informed us that the x-ray revealed, as he figured, that Mikele had a seizure in his sleep, and has little to no brain activity.

Mike and I rushed back to Mikele's room. He was attached to so many different machines that just the sight of it broke my heart and I knew at that moment what I had to do.

"We can't leave him like this. He's suffering!

"I know baby! I know! This is just so hard!"

We called the doctor in and told him what we wanted to do and made sure that our decision was the best to do.

Even though they were small Mikye and Mikele shared a bond and just like in the dream I had, I know that they would want to be together even though knowing that did not make it easier to let go.

The doctor showed us the x-rays confirming that what he said was true and that at this point only the machines were breathing for and keeping my son alive.

"You can invite the rest of your family to say goodbye if you like," the doctor said.

"No, doctor. This is something Michael and I have to do together. Okay then, a nurse and I have to be present. Whenever you are ready, you would unplug this chord," the doctor said and move to the side of the room.

I bend down to Mikele. "If you can hear me baby, I love you, I'll always love you. Please take care of you brother. As much as I want you here with me. God has something else planned for you."

I touched his hand and almost lost it. Mike came over and gave me some tissue to wipe my face after wiping his own eyes.

"Sleep on, little man and know that daddy loves you and your brother! Always and forever!"

I walked to pull the plug, and Mike did as well. He covered my small hand with his large hands and together we did one of the hardest job a parent ever have to do! It took a few minutes before the machine buzzed to let us know that Mikele was gone. Those were the longest minutes of my life. How do you count the minutes until your loved one leaves this earth? Honestly, I can't recall those minutes. I remember Mike and I pulling the plug. Then I kissed Mikele one last time and buried my head in the sheets at his bedside.

After he was gone, Mike held me and we both cried. The nurse removed all the tubes and turned off all the machine.

"I'm going to give you guys a few moments alone with him before we take him and after we have the paperwork and everything done. We will need information as to what funeral home you want to handle the arrangements," the nurse said and quickly left.

I said a short prayer for Mikele and Mikye and left. I couldn't take being in that room any longer. I ran to the bathroom near the waiting area and cried until I couldn't cry anymore.

I couldn't help but feel like this was all my fault. Like God punished my babies because of my sins. In less than twenty four hours, I had lost both of my babies. The dream of my children as angels had come true. This was one time, I wish dreams didn't come true. I know I was a horrible person, a horrible friend, but my babies were innocent. They didn't deserve to die for my sins.

"Rachel, are you okay?" I heard Mike ask while banging on the bathroom door. I don't know how long I had been in the bathroom crying.

I didn't respond. How could he ask that question? Why do people ask that question, when someone dies? *Hell no, I'm not okay. I just lost two children, not one but two. How do you think I feel?* That's what I wanted to say, but they were his children, so if anyone understood my pain, it would be him. I know he was hurting just as much as me.

"Rachel, open the door! Open the door!" Mike demanded getting louder with each word.

I opened the door and ran into his arms. Again, I cried until I couldn't cry anymore. My eyes were red and puffy and almost swollen shut. Mike and I met with the staff and made arrangements for the funeral home to come and take Mikele and

Mikye's bodies. Mike did most of the talking because I was zoned out and still in disbelief.

I couldn't take hearing the word bodies anymore, so I left out of the room. Leaving out of that room, realizing that I had to go home without my babies became too much. I felt like a zombie. My body was moving, but I didn't know how because I was hurting so bad. The pain I felt was nothing like the grief I felt when I lost my father. With each step that pain grew bigger and bigger and bigger until I felt trapped. There was nowhere else to go, I couldn't stand to go on with my life knowing that two of my kids wouldn't be here with me.

I want to die! I want to die! I want to die! I want to die! I want to die! Keep playing in my head. I wanted to die. It should have been me. I should have died instead of them. Overcome with grief, sorrow, and regret, there was only one thing left to do. I got on the elevator and when to the morgue to see my boys.

On the elevator, I sent a group text to Tammie, Persia, Sharon, my mother, and my sister explaining what I was about to do and what I wanted them to do. Then I turned off my phone and put it in my pocket.

Once I arrived at the morgue, the nurse looked at me and sensed something was wrong. I tried to perk up a little and convinced her that I just wanted to say goodbye to my boys. She still looked at me suspiciously, but she reluctantly let me in, pulled out the drawers that held my babies, pulled back the sheets, and left. They put Mikele in the drawer next to Mikye.

As I stood between my babies, tears flowed from my eyes like waves in the Pacific Ocean. *Why me? Why?* I had more tears than answers. I felt more pain than I ever thought anybody could feel. I knew what I had to do to end the pain I searched around the room for anything I could use.

I spotted a sharp-looking instrument that looked like a knife but smaller. I grabbed it. I kissed my boys one last time and started to cut my neck. Before the knife made contact with my neck, somebody grabbed my arms from behind me, causing me to drop the knife. I turned around and it was Officer Brian, Mike, and the nurse was also in the room.

While I was focusing on Brian, my eyes pleading with him to let me go, to let me just end it all and kill myself. His dark eyes pleaded with me telling me no. While our eyes were having their own conversation, the nurse snuck around and quickly stuck a needle in my arm. I fell into Brian's arms and muttered, "Why?" before everything went black.

15

MIKE

I can't believe Rachel tried to kill herself. I know dealing with Mikye and Mikele's death is hard on her because it's hard on me, but taking her life was not going to bring them back or guarantee that she would be with them.

Persia and Sharon helped me plan a small, elegant ceremony for family and close friends only since funeral services for babies have to be done quickly. Tammie wanted to help, but I wouldn't let her considering the circumstances. I also asked her not to attend the services, but she told me she was coming to be there for our children.

Instead of separate caskets, we decided on a baby blue casket trimmed with gold that was big enough for the boys to lay side by side. We had the boys dressed in white christening rompers with small, baby blue bowties. Persia found two light blue teddy bears holding a blanket and got it monogrammed with the boys' name and birthday and put it inside the casket with the boys. I figure Rachel would like them being together. Sharon blew up the twins' birth photo to stand on the easel near the casket and we had all white floral arrangements. For the ceremony, we asked everyone to wear white.

Rachel was released from the mental hospital on the day of the funeral. I had to pull some strings to get her out a day earlier, since suicide patients have to stay a minimum of seventy-two hours. I was able to get her released early with the promised of weekly meeting with the therapist.

Tammie was coming to the ceremony and I couldn't stop her so, I asked her to slip in after Rachel is already seated. We had the ceremony in the funeral home's chapel. Rachel and I were the last ones to arrive at the ceremony. Rachel's children were seated with her mother and sister. My children were seated with Persia and Sharon along with their children. Mont and Derek was seated behind Persia. I didn't see Tammie, but I knew she was there because I saw her car outside.

For most of the morning, Rachel was quiet. She cried silently on and off the entire morning before we even arrived at the funeral. I had to be strong for her, but every time I saw her cry, it hurt me. No parent should have to bury their children.

Rachel had on a white pencil dress that hugged all the right places, with royal blue pumps. She wore a baby blue corsage on her dress with a small ribbon with the boys' name. She wore big sunglasses and a black pill box church hat with netting. Even without makeup on, she was stunning.

By the time of the ceremony, she had cried so much that her eyes were swollen from the tears. When we entered the chapel, everyone was already seated. The white flowers, the all-white attire throughout the room made the baby blue and gold casket stand out beautifully. I know it was a funeral and death is never beautiful to the people that are losing their loved ones, but the setting gave everyone feelings of peace, hope, faith, and most of all love.

I grabbed Rachel's hand and we walked down the short aisle to the casket. Although the walk was only about twenty feet, it felt so much longer. A sullen feeling overtook me and I almost lost it. Reality was starting to sink in and after being strong for everyone else, I felt like I was finally about to lose it. Rachel must have sensed it and she squeezed my hand tighter. Although, it wasn't much, it meant a lot knowing that she acknowledged that I was hurting just as much as she was. The tears started falling and escaping from underneath the shades we wore.

When we reached the casket, Rachel let go of my hand and walked closer to the casket. She removed her glasses and kissed

Mikye on the cheek and then Mikele. For a few moments, she just stood there crying, staring at them. After about three minutes of her just standing there. I tried to walk her to her seat but she wouldn't move. She collapsed on the floor by the casket. I hurriedly kneeled down beside her. Her mother and kids started to get up to come to her but I put up my hand to stop them.

"Rachel? Rachel? Are you okay? Can you get up?" I asked her.

She started shaking her head and started hyperventilating like she was having an asthma attack or panic attack.

I could see the fear in her kids' faces. Rachel's mother got up and took the kids outside.

"Lift her head up into your lap and let her breath into this bag," Tammie said handing me the bag. I don't even remember seeing Tammie get up.

When Rachel saw Tammie her breathing escalated. She wanted to say something to Tammie and from the looks of it, it wasn't going to be good.

"Rachel, you have to calm down. Now breathe into the bag like you did that day at the supermarket. It's going to help regulate your breathing before you pass out."

Rachel took the bag from me, and did as Tammie said. After a few moments, her breathing slowed down and returned to normal.

Getting up off the floor, she stood by the casket once again, kissed the twins' and signaled for the funeral directors to close the casket.

"Is everything okay? Do we need an ambulance?" a police officer asked. He looked familiar, but I couldn't remember where I knew him from.

"Yes, officer. Everything is okay. She had a panic attack, but she is okay now," Tammie said to the officer.

The officer said, "Okay." Rachel looked at Tammie, but this time she didn't frown. She gave a half-smile to her and whispered to me that she wants to say something.

"We want to go ahead and get the ceremony starated. Rachel would like to say something, so can everyone take their seats and tell the other guests to come in as well," I said.

Tammie went and got Rachel's mother and kids and everyone else that stepped out when Rachel had her panic attack.

Rachel walked to the podium. She gained some strength from somewhere because even though she was still crying. She composed herself quickly and nicely. She held a tranquil pose at the podium.

"Thank you for coming today. I honestly didn't think I could do this today. Your support has been wonderful. This is simply beautiful." Rachel said and paused.

She seemed to be getting emotional again. She took a minute to get herself together and continued on.

"I don't deserve such good friends. I treated you guys really bad and when I think about it, it hurts because I hurt the main people that were trying to help me. I hurt the people that were more like family to me than actual family and for that I am truly grateful. Mikye and Mikele are at peace now. I know my daddy and my grandmother will watch over there. If I have learned anything from this is that life is short. There is no time to hold grudges or hate people. For everyone, I've hurt, I want to sincerely apologize. I'm saddened that tragedy had to invade my life for me to see all the wrong I have done and it pains me to think that my sins caused what happened with my boys, but I am working on accepting the fact that God needed them more than me. Thank you for doing this for my boys. I love you guys!" Rachel said and hurried to her seat beside me, before she completely lost it.

She laid her head on my shoulder and cried. MaKayla got up and sung a song. She sung, "Borrowed Angels," by Kristen Chenoweth. I didn't even know she knew that song and although it was the perfect song for the occasion, it hit Rachel hard. All I could do was hold her and wipe her tears, while mines flowed freely down my face. That song touched everyone. There was not a dry eye in the entire room. After she finished singing, she gave me and Rachel a hug.

The pastor was so touched and overwhelmed by the song that he could barely officiate the ceremony. I barely remember much of what the pastor was saying. I remember looking around the room and seeing everyone crying. I saw my children crying and Tammie consoling them as best she could. I saw Persia and Derek consoling their children, although it was obvious that he and Persia were not on good terms. Instead of them sitting together they sat on different pews. I saw Mont moved closer to Sharon to help console their children. It was clear that Mont wanted Sharon back, but I'm not sure that Sharon felt that way. The way he touched her hand

and the way he looked at her just screamed that he wanted her back.

Watching Mont's intimate moment with Sharon, made me think of my marriage. A part of me wanted to leave Rachel and go and be with Tammie and our kids to help comfort them, but I couldn't. Rachel had no one. Her mother and sister were comforting her kids and Rachel was alone.

I couldn't leave her especially how she broke down earlier. I've prepared myself in advance because reality truly hits you at the burial, when you watch that casket gets lowered into the vault and sealed and put into the ground. At least that's the hardest part to me.

All the children acted as flowers bearers and carried the flowers from the chapel to the cars and then from the cars to the grave. It was wonderful seeing them trying to help out. The burial went well and surprisingly, Rachel didn't break down. She left and went to the family car, when they started lowering the casket in the ground. I decided to give her some time alone, so I didn't follow her. I saw her talking to that same police officer again. He gave her something that looked like his business card or something. I guess they know each other.

The rest of the family and friends also started leaving, but I stayed until the casket was out of my sight. The pain in my chest rose with every inch the casket was lowered. I didn't want things to end like this, regardless of my situation with Rachel, I never thought I would lose my kids in the process.

I know we can't question God, but I couldn't help asking *why*? Was God punishing me and Rachel for what we did? That's how it felt. The Lord works in mysterious ways, my mother used to always say. I guess he needed Mikye and Mikele in heaven, more than Rachel and I needed them here.

As the grave diggers, prepared to cover the casket, I wiped my face and decided to join the rest of the family. I was headed over to talk to Derek and Mont, but Tammie approached me as I leave from the burial site.

"Can I talk to you for a minute?" She asked.

"Sure. What's up?"

"I'm sorry for your loss, Mike. I never meant for any of this to happen. I know this really isn't the time to talk, but I rarely see you. I'm not sure if I'll see you again, so I want you to know I filed the divorce papers. Whenever you go back to work, they will be delivered to you," she said and walked off and joined our kids that were standing with Persia, Sharon, and the rest of the kids.

I talked to Mont and Derek, briefly before we all joined the women and children. I thanked Persia and Sharon for all their help with the ceremony.

I talked to and hugged my children. It felt like I had been away from them an eternity. Regardless of what happens between Tammie and me, we have to find a way to work together for our children's sake because I missed them like crazy. I shouldn't have allowed the situation with their mother prevent me from being in their lives. I can't go back and change the past. All I can do is step up, admit my mistakes, and try to be the father, I used to be to them.

For a moment, I got this weird feeling like Mikye and Mikele death was necessary, so Rachel and I could get our lives together and start doing right by people and focusing on others instead of our selfish needs and wants. I know that sounds crazy, but Mikye and Mikele would have kept Rachel and I bonded. Feelings between the both of us would have eventually came to the surface and that would have interrupted my life with Tammie and my kids.

Don't misunderstand me, though. I love my boys. I love Mikye and Mikele just as much as I love MJ and my girls. They are my kids, and I will always love them, always. Maybe this is one of those mysterious ways that God shows us that He is God and He knows us better than we know ourselves. Even when we don't understand the plan, we have to trust in Him.

"Tammie? Can I talk to you for a minute?" I said interrupting her conversation with Persia.

"What is it, Mike?" She said with a slight attitude.

"I'm taking the kids to the movies at six," I said sternly. I was going to ask Tammie, but I didn't want to hear her smart mouth, so it was easier for me to tell her my plans than to ask for her permission to implement those plans.

***

The repast was held at Sharon's house and for a brief moment, it felt like the old days. I can't remember the the last time we were together. Sharon, Mont, Persia, Derek, Tammie, Rachel, and I. Seems like a lifetime ago, when we were all best friends and happy in love.

Friends grow apart and people fall out of love. So, even though, we were all together, you could cut the tension with a knife. Persia and Derek weren't talking to each other. Derek was trying to talk to Persia, but Persia ignored him completely and took great care to not be alone with him. Tammie avoided me because she was still mad at me about the entire situation and she didn't want to upset Rachel. Rachel wasn't crying anymore, but she also wasn't talking or socializing with anyone. She stayed in the den alone most of the time. I checked on her a time or two but she just wanted to be left alone.

Surprisingly, the only people that seemed to be enjoying each other's company was Sharon and Mont. They have been quietly flirting with each other all day. At first, I thought he was just being nice and supportive of Sharon because she and Rachel were really close, but watching them more closely, they were definitely flirting with each other.

From my understanding, Mont was gay or bisexual and that's why their marriage didn't work. I thought Sharon had moved on with Nicole. They seemed so happy and in love on the trip to Hawaii, but I haven't seen Nicole with Sharon in a while. Maybe Sharon decided to give Mont another chance.

It was getting close to six o'clock and I promised my kids, I would take them to the movies. Well my kids must have told the other kids because when I told my kids to get ready to go, all the children started getting ready. Before we even knew what had happened, Mont, Derek, and I ended up taking all the kids to the movies.

I let Rachel know that her kids were going to the movies with me and that I would bring them back to her later. As we were leaving, I saw Rachel leave out of the den and walk over and talk to Tammie. I froze in place, wondering if they were about to kill each other, but instead of pulling hair and pointing fingers, I saw them hug. It was the first step and on that note, I went out the door to enjoy the rest of the day with the guys and our children.

16

BRIAN

I felt so bad for Rachel. I couldn't even begin to imagine the pain she felt from losing not one but two children. Although, I didn't have any children of my own, I think of the kids on my football team as my own and I couldn't imagine losing any one of them.

When she tried to kill herself at the hospital, the pain I saw in her eyes. I never want to feel like that. Seeing her like that, I just wanted to hold her, wipe her tears, and make everything better. I felt so connected to her. It's like fate has been pulling us together ever since the day I saw her at Wal-Mart. I literally have been running into Rachel everywhere. I've never been one big on fate, but something was going on and even Rachel noticed it too.

We ran into each at the hospital when Chico got shot. I just happened to be in the hospital when the call came in about a distraught patient in the morgue. I was the officer assigned to the funeral procession for her children, and I was there at the chapel and the burial site.

I talked to her at the burial site for a minute and gave her my card and told her to call me whenever she needed someone to talk. Even though, I don't know her personally, I truly feel connected to her. Maybe it's because she lost twins and I've always wanted twins or maybe it's the idea that fate was bringing us together for a reason. Since we first met, Rachel always manages to occupy space in my mind. I think about her a lot. Giving her my number probably was a mistake because I am attracted to her, but I'm also a married man.

Nicole has been acting like a good wife for once in a long time. We had a magical night together but I couldn't help wondering if it was because she was guilty of something or because she really missed me when she was on her trip to Hawaii. I love Nicole but I'm ready to start a family and she does not. I'm not even sure if she even wants kids. Every time I bring up the idea, it leads to an argument with her.

I'm getting conflicted. I feel like I'm in a loveless marriage. I love Nicole but I unless we get some intense therapy or better communication, this marriage is going to continue to crumble up and die. I've never cheated on Nicole, but the fact that Rachel is on my mind so much, I feel like I'm already cheating. Whether I wanted to admit it or not, I was definitely falling for Rachel and keeping all of these feelings inside about Rachel or Nicole is slowly killing me.

I decided to talk to Chico about it and get his opinion about it. He is doing much better and insisted on going to the strip club.

As bad as I may have it for Rachel, I don't think my crush is even close to Chico's obsession over Kandi. He is in love with a stripper, but who knows, maybe he and Kandi can be like Murch and Candace from the movie, *Best Man* get married, have kids, and live happily ever after. Well, maybe not happily ever after, but live peacefully and happy. It's kind of Ironic that her actual name is Candace as well and her stripper name is Kandi just like on the movie.

Regardless of her job, I truly believe Kandi feels a little something for Chico. She even called him and visited him in the hospital when she found out that he got shot. If they could make a relationship work regardless of her job, then I'll be happy for them. In a perfect world, Chico and Kandi would be together and Rachel and I would be together.

Maybe the strip club could deter my thinking for a little while. I picked up Chico and we headed to the club. We sat at a table since it wasn't time for Kandi to perform yet. The timing was perfect because I really wanted to talk to him about this Rachel thing.

"Man, I'm getting that itch!"

"What itch man? What the hell you talking about?" Chico asked.

"To cheat on Nicole. I've never cheated on her, NEVER, but I met this woman a few weeks back and I can't stop thinking about her. I don't know what to do. The thoughts and dreams I have of this woman, make me feel like I'm already cheating on Nicole and no matter how hard I try to forget this woman, somehow, we always run into each other again. It's like our paths our meant to cross for some reason."

With a serious look on his face, Chico responded, "Wow, man! That's deep. Have you told this woman how you feel?"

"Her name is Rachel. I'm not sure how to and plus now is not the right time because she just lost her twin boys. She's taking it hard too and I just want to be there to comfort her, but I don't know how to do that."

"That's hard, but I think you should just tell her how you feel and go from there. I mean you will never know until you try. As for Nicole, man you know I stay out of your business, but you deserve better. Even I know how bad you want kids and after seven years, I'm surprised she hasn't had one or two, already. If she doesn't want kids, then I just don't see how your marriage is going to work. Also, if Rachel just lost two kids, I'm not sure if she would want kids again, either. So, before you get all deep into her and create this perfect fantasy relationship, just tell her how you feel and go from there. Now enough of all this sentimental crap! Let's get some shots and turn up and enjoy all these nice asses bouncing around her!" Chico said and laughed.

After a couple shots and a couple of lap dances, it was time for Kandi's dance. Of course, Chico had his money ready as we made our way closer to the stage. Tonight she danced to Ciara's *Body Party* and like always she didn't disappoint. Instead of working the stage like she always does, she danced mostly on the pole doing tricks up and down the poles. When she finally did dance around the stage, she paid a lot of attention to Chico.

Even though she was dancing specifically for Chico, the other men were still throwing tons of money onto the stage. She would occasionally move around the stage, so as not to disappoint her other fans, but she always made her way back to Chico. As her dance ended, she winked at Chico as security came and help her gather her cash before the next stripper came out.

My phone started vibrating in my pocket. I looked at the screen and saw a number I didn't recognize. I told Chico that I would be right back, I had a phone call. When I got outside, I called the number back.

"Hello, did someone call this number?"

"Brian, it's Rachel. Can you come over please? I don't know who else to call, but I just don't want to be alone right now."

"Okay, I'll be there. What's your address?"

"6850 Panda Ct, Austell."

"Okay, I'll be there. Just don't do anything to harm yourself. Stay on the phone with me until I get there in case I get lost. We can talk about whatever you want to talk about. Hold on a minute, let me tell Chico I'm about to go. Don't hang up!

I went back into the club, found Chico. "I'm going to see Rachel, can you find a ride home?"

"Sure, man. Go ahead and handle that, but be careful," he said.

"Ok, I'll talk to you later."

"Ok, cool!"

"Rachel, you still there?" I said into the phone.

"Yes, I'm here," she whispered into the phone.

I could tell that she had been crying and I didn't want her to try to kill herself again, so I had to keep her talking to take her mind off the way she was feeling.

"So, Rachel. Since I have no idea where I'm going. How about we play a game to keep me occupied and in the process, I learn more about you. The game is called *21 Questions*. I ask you a question, you can answer or pass, but every time you pass that's one dollar. Understand?"

"Okay!"

"Well, you can go first. So, ask me something," I said excitedly into the phone.

"Ummm mmmm, how long have you been a police officer?" She asked.

"Nine years. Okay, my turn. What's your favorite color?" I asked.

"Purple. I love the color purple. What's yours?"

"Believe it or not, my favorite color is purple. I was a Que in college, so I have to love purple. But seriously, I love purple, so that's one thing we have in common. What is your favorite food?" I asked.

"I'm a pizza lover. I probably order *Pizza Hut* at least once a week," she said. "What is your favorite food?"

"I love Chinese food. Shrimp egg rolls and Shrimp chicken fried rice, General Tso chicken, and sweet and sour chicken are my favorites. Do you have a boyfriend?

"No, I don't but I don't like this game. Let's talk about something else," she said.

"Okay. How about this? I'm almost there according to the GPS. So, put on some comfortable casual clothes and I'm take you out."

"No, that's not going to work. You're married and I have had my share of married men and the damage it causes in the end. So, I think I'm have to pass.," she said in a serious tone.

"Yes, I'm married, but I'm not trying to have sex with you tonight. I just want to make you smile because I know you are hurting inside. That's all. I just want to be a good friend tonight. So how about you decide what you want to do and that's what we will do, okay?"

"Okay. I'm sorry. I didn't mean to snap like that it's just that married men has always been bad for me. I always end up hurt, so the next man I ever give myself too will have to be single because I'm done with the side chick, baby mama drama and shit."

"I understand, I'm about to pull up, so go ahead and get dressed and meet me outside," I said and hung up the phone.

I pulled in Rachel's driveway, killed the engine, and just sat there thinking about the conflicting messages I was getting from Rachel. I couldn't tell if she was feeling me or not. I wasn't going to pressure her though. I came over to help get her mind off her boys, so that's what I plan to do.

Rachel finally came out the house in white skinny jeans, a baby blue oxford shirt with the shirt rolled up to the elbows, and gray colored sandals. She looked stunning. You couldn't even tell she was grieving. I was glad to see her smiling instead of crying.

I got out of the car to meet Rachel. We hugged and I walked her to the car and opened the door for her. I hadn't done anything like that in so long that it felt weird, but a good type of weird. It's amazing how I just wanted everything to be perfect for Rachel. I wanted to be the perfect gentlemen. I wanted to save her. The question was, would she let me be the one to save her?

Since it was so late, it really wasn't anything to do besides club, strip club, or go out to eat at some of the after-hours spot. We ended up just riding and talking. We talked about everything, even sports. Rachel was a big football and boxing fan and that was a big plus in my book. She briefly talked about her boys. She cried, but it wasn't as bad as I seen her earlier. She talked about a lawyer contacting her to sue the baby formula company for negligence, but she was undecided because no amount of money would bring back her children. I saw her getting emotional, so I pulled over and hugged her and gave her a minute to compose herself before continuing with our late night drive.

After an hour or two of talking, Rachel fell asleep. Watching her sleep, I couldn't help but imagine waking up to her every day. I could have taken her home, but I wasn't ready for the night, well morning to end, so I kept driving. I learned one thing---that no matter what, I wanted Rachel in my life.

Just as the sun started to break through the clouds, I was entering Savannah, GA. I had driven almost four hours and I was not the least bit tired. I drove to Tybee Island and parked near the beach. I watched Rachel for a while longer before gently shaking her to wake her up.

"Where are we, Brian?" she asked.

"Tybee Island in Georgia. You fell asleep and I didn't want to wake you, so I just continued driving until we got here. I figure a nice walk on the beach would be wonderful for you. So, let's go," I said getting out and walking over to the passenger side of the car and helping her out.

As we walked on the beach, holding hands, watching the sun sprint up into the sky, waking up the world while gentle waves washed up and down the beach, everything felt perfect in my life for once. My mind wasn't on Nicole, my job, or anything. The only thing that mattered at the current moment, was the fact that I was the happiest I've been in a long time.

Rachel broke the silence. "I got sand in my shoes."

"I do, too." I replied. "Hold up," I said and took my shoes and socks off and folded my pants up.

Rachel took off her sandals and we both walked barefoot in the sand.

"Surprisingly, you have pretty feet!" She said.

"What is that supposed to me? You seem shocked," I replied.

"I'm just saying, most guys don't have pretty feet."

"Well, I'm not most guys. I get occasional pedicures. You know, I got to keep my feet pretty and kissable in case, somebody want to suck some toes!" I said and laughed.

"You are crazy!" Rachel exclaimed.

We walked a little further on the beach before sitting down to cloud-watch. I laid down on my back and Rachel laid down next to me and for over thirty minutes, we analyzed the clouds and what shapes or objects they resembled.

"Sorry to interrupt this awesome session of cloud-watching, but my stomach is ready to food-watch!" Rachel stated.

"Ok, let's go before your blood sugar drop and you turn all psycho on me," I said as I got up and held out my hand to help her up.

We gathered our shoes and walked back to the car. I drove back to Savannah and since it was so early all of the coffee shops and restaurants in Savannah's historic district was closed, so we ended up going to *Waffle House.*

"So, what do you want to do after breakfast? Are you ready to get back to Austell or do you want to hang out around here a while and see what Savannah have to offer us?" I asked.

"I wouldn't mind staying a while longer. It is relaxing me, but I don't have any clothes or anything like that," she said.

"That's not a problem. I'm sure they have some great shopping stores around plus, if they don't I guarantee there's a *WAL-MART* around here somewhere," I laughed.

"Wal-Mart?" Rachel said giving me the side eye.

"Hey, don't sleep on Wal-Mart, it's one-stop shopping, lol, but if you want to visit more of the *upscale* stores and boutiques, it's going to be a few hours before they open. So, let's just go to Wal-Mart and pick up a few necessities and some beach wear and get a room and change clothes and prepare to explore Savannah, GA. We can get separate rooms or however you want to do it, is fine with me," I said.

"Brian, I trust you. You are a true gentlemen, or one hell of a pretender. Anyway, if I didn't feel comfortable with you I would have never called you, so relax. But just in case you turn out to be a serial rapist, or serial killer, I'm going to call Sharon and tell her who I'm with and give her your tag number. I know I'm dealing with a lot right now, but I don't want anyone treating me like a baby or throwing pity parties, okay?"

"Well on that note, come on woman! Let's go to Wal-Mart and get fresh!" I said laughing.

Rachel laughed with me and it was so nice to see that beautiful smile of hers again. She called Sharon, but didn't get a respond, so she left a message. We went to the store and got toiletries, beach clothing, snacks, beach supplies, and two weekend bags. Savannah was nice, but Rachel liked Tybee Island better, so we ended up getting a room at Tybee Island Bed and Breakfast, so that we could be closer to the beach. The inn was charmingly picturesque. The front yard and porch area was spectacular. There was a big, live oak in the yard with hanging Spanish moss. There was a beautiful fountain in the middle of the yard surrounded by amazing gardens creating a wonderful dappling of sun and shade.

The staff was wonderful. The receptionist greeted us at the door and showed us to the Lighthouse Room, which was the attic turned into a bedroom. It was spacious and clean. It had two beds and balcony with a private bath.

Even though, we had already eaten breakfast, the hostess insisted that we try the breakfast. I'm glad that we did, because the food was delicious. They served us Shrimp and grits with stuffed French toast.

After eating breakfast, we prepared for a fun-filled day in Tybee Island. While Rachel was changing clothes, I decided to walk around the beautiful gardens in the yard. The backyard was just as beautiful as the front. Whereas the front yard had the wraparound southern porch, the back also had a porch lined with small tables and chairs for guests that wanted to eat outside. There were more amazing gardens, and a porch swing hanging from an oak tree. There were also lounge chairs if you want to sit out in the gardens instead of on the porch. The side of the inn had picnic tables and a path that led to a beautiful, white gazebo that was used for weddings or other ceremonies. The quaint décor gave the inn such a homey feeling.

The balcony to our room overlooked the garden and when I looked up, I saw Rachel standing there watching me overlooking the yard. She had on the colorful maxi dress with sandals that we picked up at Wal-Mart earlier, but the dress fitted her curves so perfectly that unless I told you, you wouldn't believe that the dress was from Wal-Mart. When she noticed me looking at her, she smiled and walked back into the room. I admired the scenery once more before heading back inside to change clothes, so we could find something to do.

17

SHARON

I woke up to a voicemail from Rachel letting me know she was okay and that she was with Brian. She also asked if I could watch the kids for another day or so.

Now I understand why Nicole was blowing my phone up last night. Her hubby ran off with my best friend and she decided to call the rebound guy. I'm so glad, I ignored her calls and text. I'm done playing these games with Nicole. I called Rachel back to check on her and she answered on the second ring as if she was expecting my call.

"Hey Hun, I got your message. You know I'll watch the kids that's no problem. Are you okay?" I asked her.

"I'm fine. Brian is taking real good care of me and he is being such a gentlemen. I'll be home either later today or tomorrow. I'm not sure yet. I just need some time to clear my mind and stuff," Rachel replied.

"Okay, well call me if you need me. Love you girl!"

"I love you too and tell my babies, I love them and mommy will be home soon!" Rachel said and hung up.

I looked over at Mont, lying beside me. His long, untamed dreads were all over the place. His russet, reddish-brown skin looked like it was glowing and he was smiling in his sleep. I'm not sure if he was dreaming or if he was still smiling from last night.

I eased out of the bed and went into the bathroom. I had to get myself together and start making better decisions and regardless of my actions with Nicole and Mont, I think it's time for me to just really focus on myself.

I'm ready to just end things with Nicole. Every time I see her with Brian it feels as if the knife she placed in my heart goes deeper and deeper. She still hasn't said anything about Hawaii. Although, I already know she cheated on me, she still hasn't admit it or apologized. I can't be mad at her, though. It's my fault, so starting today I'm going to start moving on with my life and leave her and her happy marriage alone; however, Mont wants to be a family again and as much as the kids enjoy having him around, I'm done with him also. I'm no longer going to hide who I am to make others feel better about themselves. If someone truly loves you, they would love you just as you are and if they don't then you have to love yourself enough to let them go! I know that's easier said than done, but as of today, I'm making the first step towards my happiness.

Last night was a mistake. We were both emotional and had a little bit too much to drink after the kids went to bed or maybe it was because he really stepped up to the plate and was there for me and the kids at the funeral.

I got dressed and went downstairs to start breakfast before everyone woke up. Just as I walked into the kitchen, there was a knock at the door.

"Who is it?" I asked.

"Nicole."

I opened the door and Nicole was standing there filled with attitude.

I walked onto the porch with Nicole closing the door behind me, so that I didn't wake the kids or Mont up.

"Nicole, you got some nerves coming over here with an attitude! You have placed me on the backburner ever since we got back from Hawaii and now you realize that your marriage isn't as squeaky clean as you thought it was. You want to run over here. You realize that Brian isn't going to be your little puppet anymore like you thought that I would be, but you are wrong. Yes, I got your calls and text last night, I just ignored them, kind of like the way you have been ignoring me. So, please stop the act like you care when you don't because you see, I know you cheated on me in Hawaii. I was just hoping that you would be woman enough to tell me and apologize, but you couldn't could you? Then you get back to Georgia and act like I don't even fucking exist! I didn't come out of the closet, just so you can put me back in one because you still standing in the doorway of your own closet. You so used to having things your way, that you couldn't stop and realize when someone really loves you. I'm done playing games with you. Matter of fact, I'm done with you. I love you, Nicole. I'll always love you, but I love myself more and I refuse to continue to play second fiddle and let you play with my heart. You and I both know that you didn't come over her because you loved me. You came over here because you were hurt about Brian and you were angry that I ignored you, well get used to that feeling, because that how you make the people in your life feel all the time. It doesn't feel good do it? I know because that's exactly how I felt at the hospital. Anyway, I have to go. Goodbye, Nicole," I said and went back in the house and locked my door leaving her on my stoop.

I walked into the kitchen and started taking things out the fridge to cook for breakfast when I heard the sound of glass shattering. Mont must heard it too because he ran downstairs and out the door and I followed.

Nicole had thrown a brick through Mont's car window and was about to throw one through my window, but Mont grabbed her arms and stopped her. She finally dropped the brick and started cursing Mont and myself out.

"Oh, that's why you done with me, so you can go back to your punk ass ex-husband!" Nicole screamed.

When she said that, Mont knocked her to the ground. "Shut the fuck up! You better get the fuck out of here before things get really bad!"

She hopped up and ran to my face and started shouting obscenities. Nicole and I argued back and forth for a few minutes until the police came. After telling the officers what happened, Nicole was arrested for disturbing the peace and vandalism. She refused to go down quietly. She starting hollering threats and cursing, just causing a really big scene.

The Police finally got her handcuffed and started putting her in the car, when she looked at Mont and yelled, "You go regret what you did! I promise you that!" One of the officers put her in the car, while the other officer got more information from Mont and me.

When the police finally left, I texted Rachel and let her know what happened and got started with breakfast, surprisingly the incident didn't wake the kids up.

"Your girlfriend is crazy!" Mont said while sitting at the kitchen island watching me cook.

"She's not my girlfriend."

"Well, somebody forgot to give her that memo," stated Mont.

"I gave her the memo, when she first got here and that's why she went all crazy because she think I broke up with her for you."

"Well, since she already thinks that, why not give us another chance?"

"Mont, we been through this. I'm sorry, last night shouldn't have happened. You are who you are and I am who I am and us being together is not going make that go away."

"Sharon, I'm not asking you to hide who you are. I just want my family back. Our children should grow up with both of their parents."

"You are asking me to live a lie and I just can't do that. I'd rather be alone and be happy than content and living a lie. Let's be real, Mont. You know that would never work. I have no problem with us co-parenting, but that's all I have to offer. Now, go wake the kids up for breakfast."

"Fine, Sharon. Just know that I love you and I will always love you. Oh, and last night was amazing! Since you already shot me down, how about one more time for the road," he said while walking behind me and wrapping his arms around my waist.

"Um, no! Not go happen, now please go wake the kids."

18

TAMMIE

The funeral for Mikye and Mikele was yesterday. Persia and Sharon did a wonderful job on the decorations. Rachel had a panic attack, but she managed to make it throw the entire ceremony. Her strength was unwavering. I couldn't never understand how she felt and what she felt burying her children.

I wouldn't say that Rachel and I are best friends or even friends at all, but she hugged me and that's a start considering we haven't really talked in months.

Mike picked the kids up this morning to spend some time with him, which gave me the house to myself for a while and all I wanted to do was relax, but being alone was giving me too much time to think about the mistakes I've made in my life. I had to get out of the house, so I decided to go for a run.

I haven't walked or ran at the soccer fields since before the incident between Jamal and I, out of fear that I would bump into him. Since it was later in the morning, I figured the track would not be so packed. So, I got dressed and went to the field for a morning run. As expected, there wasn't many people there, so I was able to relax a little. Even though, Jamal apologized and said he was getting help, the events of that day and how he just completely snapped on me, still played in my mind. While making my second lap around the field, I noticed a guy that looked similar to Jamal, but I brushed it off and kept running. As I stopped to get some water, I realized that it was Jamal and he was headed my way.

Of course, my guard went up, but the smile on his face and the light shining in my eyes, making his brown eyes appear hazel were warming up my heart.

"Hey, Tammie. I haven't seen you here in forever," he said.

"I know. I started going to Anytime Fitness." *Why did I tell him what gym I went to?*

"I'm sorry. I keep acting like what happened between us, didn't happen. You stopped coming because of me. I get it, I'm sorry. Tammie, you just have to know how sorry I am. Give me a chance to make it up to you, please," Jamal pleaded.

"I'll think about it!"

"Well, my number is the same. Nice seeing you again, Tammie," Jamal said before walking away and hitting the track.

After that, I didn't feel much like exercising anymore, so I left and went home. For a couple hours, I binged watched old episodes of *Prison Break*, but my mind was in overdrive.

My mind fell on Jamal. Once upon a time, I was sure that I would spend the rest of my life with him and for a short time, we were happy until he flipped out on me. I'm not going to say it wasn't his fault, but I'm glad that I understand now why things happened the way they did.

I decided to call Jamal and invite him to a late lunch. I probably shouldn't jump back out there so soon after just filing for divorce from Mike, but who's to say I can't have a little fun until I decide my next move.

He answered on the fourth ring.

"Hello, Jamal. It's me, Tammie. Before you say anything, just be quiet and listen. I'm having a real bad case of cabin fever and if I don't get out of this house, I am going to go crazy. The thing is I don't feel like being alone, so would you like to accompany me to a late lunch? Since I'm asking, I'll even pay."

"Hello, Tammie. I would love to go to lunch with you but I'm not used to women treating me, so as the man, I'll plan a fun-filled evening for us and all you have to do is show up. So meet me at Piedmont Park at the entrance near the parking garage at four. I can finally get a chance to show you how sorry I am for everything I did to you."

*****

I wore a strapless peach linen maxi dress with brown sandals and a floppy straw hat with a brown bow in the back. Summers in Atlanta were harsh. The dry heat is sometimes unbearable, so I wore something that I would be cool in and not too overdressed.

I parked and walked to the entrance of the park and sat on the bench waiting on Jamal to arrive. After a few minutes, Jamal showed up in khaki cargo shorts and a white fitted tee with a pair of charcoal Levi's men casual sneakers. He had on black and silver aviator shades that hid his sexy dark brown eyes and he had diamond stud earrings in both ears.

He looked like he was going to a summer photo shoot. Women were looking and some were trying their hardest to get his attention. I felt a little bit jealous. I wanted to walk over to Jamal and kiss him to make the other women jealous and just to taste his lips, because he was definitely looking good enough to eat.

He finally spotted me out of the crowd and came over. He hugged me and his *Dolce & Gabbana Intenso* cologne attacked my nose and I almost melted in his arms, but I resisted the urge. I was so keen on his attire and his look that I hadn't noticed the picnic basket he held in his hand until the handle poked me in the back.

"I'm sorry. Instead of going to a restaurant, I figured we could maybe have a nice picnic in the park."

"That's fine, a picnic would be wonderful! Come on, let's go find a great spot to set up," I said.

I must admit, being with Jamal, those feelings from before were starting to resurfaced and I didn't know what to do. The incident with him the last time we were together had me extra careful about giving my heart to him, again.

We found a nice spot to have our picnic near the picnic shelter in the park. The park wasn't too packed today. Jamal spread his Georgia Bulldogs fleece throw on the ground, so we could sit down. Then he started unpacking the basket, which was filled with plastic containers. He had strawberries, grapes, watermelon cubes, pasta salad, turkey wrap sandwiches, chocolate chip cookies, and my favorite candy *Turtles*.

We ate lunch and talked. We talked about everything from the weather to politics. The more I got to know about him. It was refreshing to talk about something other than what happened between us. As we started to get things together to go, he pulled an envelope from the basket and handed it to me.

I opened the envelope and pulled out an *I'm sorry* card. The card had a picture of a pug on the front with sad eyes and the words *I'm Sorry*. The card read, *I know I was wrong, and I feel very heavy in my heart about hurting you, nothing else can ease it more than my SORRY and your smile. At times, we say and do things which we really don't mean, please forgive me!*

"Jamal, that was sweet, but I forgave you a long time ago. You can't move forward, if you are still stuck in the past. You just got to forgive yourself."

"Thanks, Tamm. I guess I just needed to hear you say it. Can I be honest for a minute? You don't have to respond, but I have to say this. I still love you, Tammie. In fact, I never stopped loving you. Running into you the other day and now being here with you is like a dream come true! When I was in rehab, your love got me through some of my darkest moments. Tammie, you are a wonderful person. You inspire others, even when you don't know you are. Keep being awesome, Tamm. Don't ever lose that because that is what makes you!"

"Awwwww. Thanks, Jamal. Honestly, I don't be trying to be a leader. I just try to be there for others as I would want someone to be there for me."

"And that's the thing, you are always there! You didn't have to give me a second chance, but you did and for that I will be forever grateful."

We finished packing up the picnic and walked around the park for a while, before deciding to check out the summer jam sessions in Centennial Park. Every Thursday evening, they have musicians and bands play music in the park during the evenings.

Jamal got the blanket and we found a spot on the ground among the other people at the park. Some were in chairs, but majority were like us, sitting on blankets. The event had already started by the time we arrived and as we were finishing, a local country singer was finishing up.

The emcee introduced a lady by the name of Grande`
Beauty. She was going to do spoken word. Everyone got quiet
thinking, *what is she about to do and I hope she is good.* She was a
gorgeous, plus-sized woman, with long curly tresses. She had on a
white casual shirt with a long, flowing, black and white polka-dot
maxi skirt.

I had heard about her sultry poetry since I've been living in
Georgia, but I never attended one of her shows. Finally getting a
chance to see her perform was going to be awesome.

"I've always wanted to see her perform!"

"I remember you talking about her when we first met.
Guessed we lucked out today!"

"Yes, today has been wonderful, Jamal. You get some
brownie points!" I said while laughing. "But for real, thank you! I'm
truly enjoying myself and this small break away from the kids!"

"You're welcome, now be quiet so I can enjoy Miss Grandè
Beauty!"

I laughed at Jamal and we both started watching the show,
when a woman approached us and stopped.

"Hey, Jamal! Long time, no see or hear from!" The lady said with much attitude in her voice which cause me to sit up straight just in case something popped off. I had been leaning back onto Jamal's chest on the blanket.

"TAMEKA! What the hell do you want?" Jamal exclaimed while standing up.

"Now, is that anyway to talk to the mother of your child and someone you once loved so much?" She replied while looking directly at me.

I see now she was looking to get something started. So, I stood up next to Jamal and looked at him. My eyes telling him, that he better do something and he'd better do it quick because my patience was running out and I wasn't going to be quiet much longer, if she kept pushing.

"You mean the woman that killed my child and made me hate her? Maybe, you mean the woman that tried to kill herself? Which one you mean? Because from my knowledge, I left them all!"

Tameka was taken aback by Jamal's comment, but before she could respond, Jamal continued.

"Tameka, you and I have nothing to talk about. Please save the act, because Tammie knows about you and your little game is not going to work here. So, do us both a favor, save yourself the embarrassment, and get the fuck out of my face!"

She wanted to respond, but instead walked away. I looked at Jamal, pulled him to me, and kissed him. When we finally separated our lips, Jamal hugged me and whispered in my ear.

"Alright, don't get nothing started, you can't finish!"

I whispered back to him and said, "I love a challenge, remember?"

We caught the end of Grandè's performance and she brought the house down her spoken word was about women's empowerment and the women in the crowd were going crazy.

Because we missed most of her performance, I asked Jamal to come with me so we can see if we would get a chance to meet her around the stage area. Imagine my surprise when she was selling autographed copies of her spoken word cd, *Memoirs of a Sultry Poetess*. I got me a signed copy of her cd and she even took a picture with me.

We stayed and watched a few more acts before finally leaving. I wasn't ready to leave but Mike texted that he would be bringing the kids back home soon.

Jamal drove me back to my car and we said our goodbyes with a lot of kissing and rubbing. Driving home, my mind drifted back to the night that Rachel had the twins. The feeling I felt when I ran into his arms. The feeling when I looked up at the star in the sky. The closeness I felt and how complete, he made me feel. I felt that when the twins were born. Now the twins are gone and Jamal has somehow managed to make me feel that way again. Things work out in mysterious ways, because I never saw any of this happening.

With Mike and me definitely divorcing this time, all I know is that it's time to stop looking back and move forward with my life and who knows, maybe Jamal has finally got everything together again. I loved him once, maybe, just maybe, I can love him again!

19

PERSIA

Thank God we all made it through the funeral. Death is never easy and it's even harder when it's the death of a child. Considering the circumstances, I would say Rachel did well at handling the funeral and everything minus the suicide attempt hiatus earlier, it seemed like she was actually coming to terms with Mikye and Mikele's death.

For a brief moment, we were all together again. Just a split second, a short moment in time, the *EXQUISITE DIVAS* were back together again. The issues among ourselves didn't matter. Our issues in our relationships and marriages didn't matter. Nothing mattered but supporting Rachel and embracing the moment because as we saw with the twins, life is short! Not only were the girls together again, but the guys really stepped in and was very supportive throughout this entire ordeal. Mike, Mont, and Derek was there every step of the way despite the relationship issues going on. Matter of fact, I can't believe I let Derek crash on the sofa last night.

After him and the other guys took the kids out after the funeral, they got in late and the kids were not ready for him to leave, so I let him stay, but he slept downstairs. It was taking everything in me, not to wake him up and ask him to leave, but I decided to push all my anger aside and just let him stay awhile longer since he was leaving to go back on the road today. I didn't ask him about his living arrangements for two reasons, because I didn't want to know and because I was afraid of the answer.

***

I'm up cooking breakfast and since this is the kids' last day with him before he hits the road again for work and go back to wherever he is staying, I'm going to let him spend the day with the kids, but I'm going to do a little shopping and maybe make plans with Deniji for later.

The last time I was with Deniji, everything got so serious, but my night with him was magical and just what I needed. People always tell you about the aggressiveness of Nigerians, but never mention how loving some of them can be. I do have feelings for Deniji. I'm still afraid to label it yet, but it's something there, no matter how hard I try to fight it.

Just as my mind is about to take off and go into overdrive, Derek walks into the kitchen and sits down at the kitchen table.

"Good morning! Thanks for letting me stay over with the kids. I really appreciate it."

"No problem. Regardless of what we go through, you are still their father and I will never take that away from you. You are a wonderful father. Now being a good husband, is a completely different thing, but that's in the past and I really don't care to conjure up that time in our lives. I forgive you for everything, Derek and I pray that you have forgiven me also, but we will never be together again as husband and wife or boyfriend and girlfriend. Those days are done and the only relationship, I want to have with you is co-parenting."

"Thanks fine with me Persia. I deserved that and I can respect that," Derek said and then got up and went back into the living room.

I guess I kind of hurt his feelings, but I just needed to go ahead and get everything out before he got any crazy ideas in his head. I'm tired of this roller coaster relationship, up and down, together then broken up. Most of my life, my decisions have been based off of other people. For once, I am going to start living in the moment and live for myself.

I finished breakfast and called everyone for breakfast. For once in a long time, we were together as one big happy family. Even though, it was a lie, we did look good together.

After breakfast the kids got dressed to spend the day with their dad and I started cleaning up, since it was still early and I didn't have any plans. Once, the kids were gone with their father, I decided to put on some clothes and head to the mall. I wasn't planning on being at the mall long, so I threw on a pair of black tights and a fitted white t-shirt with some black yoga pants and turquoise/black Nike running shoes.

The mall wasn't crowded. I saw a lot of senior citizens exercising around the mall, but most people were at home or work instead of the mall. The best way to shop, in my opinion.

Aldo was having a huge sale and as they say, a girl can never have too many pairs of shoes, especially heels! I spotted some peach yellow pointy toe pumps that were just too cute, not to purchase. Turns out they had fuchsia, pink, and blue in stock. I got all four pairs. Just as I was about to try on a pair of black high heels sandals, my phone started ringing. I didn't recognize the number, but I answered it anyway, in case it was Derek or one of the girls.

"Hello, sexy lady!" The voice said as soon as I answered. He was trying his best to talk without using his accent, but I could still hear it. I knew then that it was Deniji.

"Hi, Deniji. Nice try, but you can't hide that accent. What's up?"

"Well, I was wondering if you would do me the honor of going to lunch with me."

"A girl could eat and since you are offering...I guess I can go."

"Stop playing! You know you just been dying waiting to hear from me! Anyway, I was thinking we could go to this soul food place in Lithia Springs called *Annie Mae's*. I'm tired of eating Chinese, African, Caribbean, and just fast food in general. I got a taste for some down south homemade cooking. So what do you say?"

"That does sound good. I'm already out. I'm at the mall at Cumberland, so how about you meet me here and I can ride with you to the restaurant."

"Okay, cool that works for me. See you soon, sexy!" Deniji said before hanging up the phone.

I finished trying on that high heels sandals and decided to get that pair as well. I paid for the shoes and went and put them in my trunk and window shopped until Deniji texted that he was about to pull up outside near the front entrance.

I went outside to wait on Deniji. After a minute or so, he pulled up in his royal blue BMW Alpina B5. I got in and Deniji greeted me with a kiss and we left. Deniji had on his glasses today and I swear, if it's possible, he looked sexier. He started wearing contacts a couple of weeks back, but seeing him in his glasses reminded me of the first time I saw him. He had on a white polo shirt with fitted blue jeans and white high top forces. I couldn't help but smile.

"What you smiling about?" he asked.

"Just happy to see you!"

"Aww. I feel special!" Deniji said with a big smile.

"You are special, Deniji!"

"You are special to me, also," Deniji stated before grabbing and kissing my hand.

We rode the rest of the way in silence, but once we got to the restaurant and Deniji parked. I leaned in and kissed him. I wanted to do that ever since he pulled up. We finally stopped kissing and went inside the restaurant. There was a small line, but the food looked delicious. They had yams, collard greens, cream corn, mashed potatoes, green beans, black eyed peas, rice, macaroni & cheese, fried okra, corn on the cob, baked chicken, fried chicken, meatloaf, ox tails, neck bones, catfish, country fried steaks, meatballs, rolls, homemade biscuits, and cornbread, and ham with an array of desserts like sweet potato pie, pecan pie, German chocolate cake, carrot cake, and lemon cake.

By the time, they got to us, I knew what I wanted. I ordered collard greens, yams, baked chicken, corn bread with sweet potato pie and sweet tea. Deniji ordered the ox tails with black eyed peas and fried okra with pecan pie and sweet tea.

We found a booth near the back of the restaurant to sit down. We had a nice conversation while we ate until the waitress walked up to seat a couple at the booth next to us. When she moved to the side, I was surprised to see who it was. Deniji must saw the surprised look on my face and turned around at well. You could cut the tension with a knife.

"Hey Persia! Keshia said.

"Hey Keshia. Antwan."

"Hey Persia. Deniji," Antwan said and hurriedly took his seat.

The nurse sensing the tension in the air asked them if they were okay with this booth or did they want to move. I was praying Antwan would want to move, but he told the waiter that they were fine where they were.

I had a feeling that things were about to go left real quick. Keshia didn't seem to mind the drama. She kept flirting with me with her eyes. I know what happened between us, but shit that was a one-time thing. Antwan was looking pissed off at the fact that Deniji and I was together and Deniji was being petty rubbing the shit in Antwan's face. He started talking loudly about what he had planned for us to do today.

Deep inside, I wanted to laugh, but I knew he was only trying to make Antwan mad, so I asked him to stop.

"Don't do that," I whispered to him.

"Ok! Now give me a kiss," Deniji demanded.

I wasn't sure if he was still fucking with Antwan or if he really wanted a kiss. He must read my mind because he responded, "Seriously, I really do want a kiss."

I leaned over the table and kissed Deniji. When we stopped, I told Deniji I was ready to go. I didn't want to hurt Antwan anymore that he was already and because Keisha wouldn't stop staring at me. She made me completely uncomfortable because I wasn't sure if she told Antwan about us or not.

Regardless, I didn't want to leave things so tense. As we prepared to leave, I stopped at Antwan and Keisha's booth.

"It was nice seeing you guys again. Take care."

"You too, Persia," Keisha said. Antwan didn't say anything, he just nodded his head and Deniji and I left.

"Where are we going now?" I asked Deniji.

"I think I'm going to take you to one of my favorite places in Georgia."

"Where's that?"

"You'll see, now buckle up!" He commanded.

We ended up at Sweetwater Creek Park. I can't remember if I ever told Deniji that this was one of my favorite places as well. Derek and I took the kids her regularly. We would barbeque or get on the paddle boats, play Frisbees or just sit on a blanket and watch the activities going on in the park.

"I love this place! I used to come here all the time with my kids and Derek," I stated to Deniji.

"Really! Cool! Have you ever been hiking on the trail?"

"No. I always wanted to, but the kids were scared of hiking and my husband, I mean Derek was never much interested in going."

Deniji parked. "Today is your lucky day! Let's go!"

He popped his trunk and took out a backpack.

"And where you going with that?" I asked him.

"WE—are going hiking today! Don't worry, we only going to do the *Red Trail*. It is only one mile one way, but it's something I want you to see on the trail. Don't worry, I got water and other supplies in my backpack, guess in case. You're going to love it, I promise. Come on," he said reaching out for my hand.

I grabbed his hand and we started on the Red Trail stopping occasionally to look at some of the small animals and birds, taking selfies, and other pictures. We saw a hummingbird drinking from a flower. The humming bird, such a majesty creature, had shades of blue, green, and pink in its feathers. Deniji snapped pictures and after a moment, the bird flew backwards from the flower and flew away. It flew away so gracefully, that I was completely in awe!

The trail's scenic view was simply breath-taking. It gave me a warm, reserved, tranquil feeling. As we neared the one-mile mark, the Red Trail ends and interacts with the White Trail. I thought we were going to start back down the Red Trail to the starting point, instead we started on the Yellow Trail.

"I thought you said we were only going to hike the Red Trail."

"I want to show you something it's not much further, I promise. Do you want to take a break?" Deniji asked.

"No, I'm just making sure you not taking me out into the boondocks to kill me or something."

"Well, I want to do something to you, but it's definitely not to kill you! The only reason I haven't done it yet is because I don't want anyone catching us and we go to jail for indecent exposure in a state park," Deniji said laughing.

"Well, how about a sample of what you want to do to me?"

Deniji pulled me to his and covered my mouth with his and kissed me, long, hard, and deep. While he kissed me, he rubbed down my back and around to my lower stomach and eased his hands into my tights. He pulled me closer while his fingers played inside of my underwear. He pulled me closer as his fingers went deeper and deeper inside me, causing me to melt like M&Ms in his hand. Just as I was about to discharge my love juice all over his fingers, I saw a couple headed towards us.

"People are coming!" I said to Deniji.

He removed his hand out of my pants and wrapped them around me as if we were hugging until the couple passed us. We broke apart and once the couple was out of sight. Deniji took his fingers that he fingered me and placed them in his mouth sucking and licking each finger.

"You taste so good!" Deniji said and grabbed my hand and pulled me off the trail into the woods, out of view.

We stopped near a huge tree about five hundred yards from the trail. Deniji removed his backpack, opened it, and pulled out a black fleece throw and laid it near the tree.

"Lay down and take off your pants and panties."

I did as I was told and Deniji picked back up right where we stopped on the trail; kissing me and allowing his fingers to explore inside me. Right before I was about to spurt, Deniji removed his fingers and replace them with his lips. He devoured my pussy with tongue like he was trying to spell his name inside of me, all thirteen letters. Deniji kept going and going until I couldn't take it anymore. He pulled down his pants and rammed his dick inside of me. Because I was so wet already, he slide right in and went as deep as he could. As he pumped his dick inside of me, I grinded my hips upwards to meet his rhythm and after a while we both exploded together.

After catching our breaths and getting cleaned up with the wet wipes that Deniji had in his backpack. We both grabbed water from the backpack to quench our thirst. Then, we packed up and made our way back to the trail.

We walked back to the car hand in hand. Whether I want to admit it or not, I was falling hard for Deniji. As I'm deep in my happy thoughts, Deniji leans over and kiss me on the neck.

I knew right then and there that I wanted to be with Deniji. Not saying I'm ready to pick out china patterns and monogrammed towels, but I'm willing to take things slowly.

20

RACHEL

It still seems unreal! Did I really just buried my babies? I feel like I'm still dreaming and I'm going to wake up and Mikele and Mikye will still be here.

I know God don't make any mistakes, but honestly I just can't help feeling as if it is my fault. I have cried so much that I can't cry anymore. Not in front of people anyway, the pity look on their faces only makes me feel worse, so I learned to cry and grieve in private.

I know everyone means well and they want to help anyway they can but it tends to hurt me more than help me. My friends and family don't know what to say to comfort me. The look on their faces when they ask if I am ok, do I need anything, or how I'm doing just makes me feel worse and all I want to do is break down.

It's true what people say. The pain of losing a child is unbearable and no one truly knows how you feel unless they have been in that situation. I don't even know how I got to the point where my eyes are not swollen from the tears. That day at the hospital, I wanted to die. I wanted to go with my babies. I'm glad I didn't get a chance to kill myself. I still have three other children that need me. Shit, their fathers don't even attempt to be in their lives and if Brian hadn't stopped me, they wouldn't have a mother either.

I'm still working through that situation. I'm not suicidal anymore, but the guilt and shame along with the grief and sorrow eats at me sometimes.

I'm truly thankful for Brian, though. He is the one that stopped me from killing myself. Well, the nurse at the mortuary, too. I guess she saw the look of surrender on my face and called for help. Brian got there right as the blade was about to make contact with my skin. Not only that, he was there for me at the funeral, burial site, and later that night when I had the breakdown and didn't know who to call.

I'm not sure if it is because of my loss or because he really likes me, but God won't send me *somebody else's husband* and I know that. The fact that he was there though, means a lot.

He is so considerate and he has been wonderful to me these last few weeks, especially in the last twenty-four hours. I have smiled and laughed more in the last day than I have in the last month, but I am holding steadfast to my vow about married men.

Getting away from it all if only for a day has been uplifting and the fact that Brian is really a nice gentleman that has not tried to take advantage of the situation, means a lot, but if were to have any chance at a relationship, he will have to be single, separated, or divorce. Also, for the first time, I am going to hold out on the *cookie*. Giving away the cookie, never worked well for me anyway, so maybe holding out will because I'm done being the side chick or fuck buddy. I want something real. I want a man that I can call my own instead of always sharing one with someone else.

Being here with Brian has put a lot of things into perspective for me. It has made me consider my options and all the things I need to do to get my life back on track and at a place, where I can truly be at peace and be happy.

My phone starts vibrating taking me away from my thoughts. I left off the balcony and went inside to get my phone. It was a text from Sharon telling me that she had called the police on Nicole for disturbing the peace and vandalizing Mont's car. She also mention that Nicole was arrested. I texted her back to let her know that I got her message, but that I was not going to tell Brian. If Nicole was in jail, I'm sure she would be calling Brian on her own.

No sooner had I finished texting Sharon, Brian comes into the room pissed. I was sure that Nicole had called him and that's why he was upset.

"What's wrong, Brian?"

"Just got a call from my friend Chico, the one that was in the hospital, telling me that my wife, Nicole has been arrested for disturbing the peace and vandalism at her girlfriend's house. I didn't even know she had a girlfriend. So, not only was she cheating on me, but she was cheating on me with a woman," Brian stated in a pissed off tone.

"Well, Brian look at it from her point of view. All she know is that you didn't come home last night."

"I understand what you are saying, but before I met you, I never even talked to or flirted with another woman. I don't know what it was about you that made me want to talk and flirt, but I've been attracted to you ever since that night at Wal-Mart. The way Chico was talking is like her and this woman has been going together for a long time. He looked at the report, but he wouldn't give me the details because he felt that I should talk to my wife about it," Brian said.

"Well, since you being honest and things are already crazy enough. I have a confession to make. I know who Nicole is cheating on you with!"

Brian eyes got big and a look of confusion filled his face.

"I'm only telling you this because you are going to find out one way or another and I don't want you thinking I had anything to do with it."

"Just tell me Rachel, because my mind is filling up with crazy scenarios. Nicole is or was dating my best friend Sharon. I found out at the hospital, but I didn't want to get involved. Plus, I really wasn't concentrating on whatever they had going on. My main focus was on my children."

Before Brian could respond, his phone rang. The expression on his face, let me know that it was Nicole calling him from jail. He got up and walked onto the balcony to answer the call. I don't know what she was saying on the other end of the phone.

I heard Brian say, "You should have thought about that before you did what you did! Call your girlfriend, call Sharon, maybe she'll drop the charges because I'm not getting you out!"

Brian turned his phone off, put it on the night stand, and started walking towards the bathroom to take a shower. He turned around and walked to me and kissed me, passionately. I got lost in his lips before he broke the kiss and went into the bathroom to shower.

I was speechless! I expected him to be angry at me or something, but he wasn't. Brian took a shower and got dressed.

"Okay, let's go enjoy the day on the beach! I'm ready to have some fun!" he said to me while gathering the things for the beach. We decided to walk to the beach instead of driving, since it was only a couple of blocks away.

Brian held my hand while we walked, but he was quiet. I decided to break the silence.

"So, you not going to talk about what just happened?"

"There's nothing to talk about. In the back of my mind, I knew she was cheating on me. The constant late night meetings, occasional business trips, and her unwillingness for us to start a family. I knew it. I think I always knew it, I just didn't want to know. I guess I figured if I did everything I was supposed to do, then she would realize just how much I loved her and we would make it.

I know that was wishful thinking. Anyway, no point in dwelling on that, she made her choice and I respect that, so it is what it is. Now come on, let's enjoy the beach," Brian said.

We arrived at the beach and set up in a spot not too far from the water. Brian rubbed sunscreen on my back and I put some on his. His skin was so smooth that for a moment, thoughts of me kissing up and down his back invaded my mind.

"Come on let's get in the water!" Brian said while pulling me up.

"I can't swim!"

"Well, I know how to swim and I promise I won't let anything happen to you."

"Ok, fine!"

Just as we were about to get into the water, I saw a lady sitting on a blanket to my right with twins boys that were about two or three years old. Immediately, my mind went back to my boys and for a brief second, her boys looked like Mikele and Mikye. I was so focused on the boys that I hadn't even noticed that I was walking towards the woman and her boys.

Brian pulled me to him and walked me back to our blanket. As soon as I sat down, everything I had been holding in for the last week came out. The tears fell fast and hard and the gut-wrenching pain I felt made me nauseous. Reality was setting in that my boys were really gone!

I cried into Brian chest until my tear ducts ran out of tears. He didn't know what to say, so he just held me and let me get everything out. After crying for about ten minutes, my eyes were puffy and I knew they were fireball red.

I got myself together as best as I could because people were starting to stare and I didn't want them thinking Brian did something to me. Once I got myself together, Brian gathered our things and we headed back to the inn.

After we got back to the room I laid down and Brian laid beside me and held me until I fell asleep. I awoke at two am hungry and thirsty as hell. On the table was a carryout plate and a bottle of water. I didn't see the note until I sat down.

You slept through lunch and dinner, so I left this in case you wake up hungry, thirsty or both! Brian

I looked over at Brian. He was sleeping so peacefully. I guess when I got up, I pulled the covers off him and the bed sheet had fallen down a little exposing his sexy, hairless chest, and two of his protruding abs.

In my mind, I was wishing that the covers would fall just a little bit more and give me a glimpse at what he was working with. I went to the bathroom and washed up and ate. After I ate, I walked onto the balcony. The sounds of the night were so soothing. I heard owls hooting, frogs croaking, crickets chirping, and other nocturnal animals. The sky was full of stars, lighting up the sky, as if it about to break dawn.

As a child, I loved looking up at the stars and as an adult, I can't even remember the last time I paid attention to them. Tonight, I couldn't stop glazing at the stars; I felt a connection to them. It was as if we both were speaking a language that no one knew but us; although, we spoke no words. Maybe it was just because in the city, no one has time to star-glaze and because the lights from buildings drown out the sky, which makes it harder to even see the stars.

I closed my eyes for a moment and a sense of calmness, peace, and love surrounded me as if someone wrapped me in a big, warm blanket. I opened my eyes and I swear for a moment, it looked like I saw something fly away. At that exact moment, I heard my grandmother's voice in my head saying, *I'm always with you and I will look after my grandbabies.* It's crazy I know, but I swear I could hear her as plain as day. I closed my eyes again and inhaled. Again, I felt a warm, secure blanket around me, only this time it was Brian.

I fell back into his arm as he wrapped his arms around me and kissed me on my neck. We stayed like that for a long time, before he grabbed my hand and let me back to bed. We laid with my back to his chest and my ass into his crotch. Once again, he wrapped his arms around me and kissed me on my neck. I turned to face him and kissed him while wrapping my legs around his waist. Brian kissed me while pushing me onto my back.

"Brian, I can't do this. Being with somebody else's husband is what started all this mess in the first place and plus I'm not trying to be your rebound or revenge fuck just because you mad at your wife."

Brian stopped kissing me and looked dead in the eyes and stated, "First of all, I'm not mad at my wife. We have been having issues for a while, so I'm not surprised that she was cheating on me.

I'm just surprised that it was with a woman. Secondly, I don't think of you as a revenge fuck or rebound. I'm not trying to fuck you. I just want to taste you. I just want to lick all your pain away. I'm sorry for being so blunt, but being here with you and not being able to taste you is driving me crazy! If you want me to stop, I will but I will hold you in my arms until we both fall asleep! Rachel, I want to be with you with or without sex, so if you want to wait, that's fine with me. Don't question whether my feelings are real because they are. I think it's safe to say, I wouldn't be here if you felt threatened by me. So, how about this....We just cuddle tonight."

Brian pulled me close to him and wrapped his arms around me until I fell asleep. I woke up the next morning to flowers on the nightstand. I reached for Brian but he was gone. I searched around the room, to make sure he hadn't left me alone in the middle of the night.

"Looking for me?" Brian said emerging from the bathroom. He startled me, but my heart skipped a beat, knowing that he was still here and that he wasn't mad about last night.

"Yes, I thought you were gone!" I said to him.

"Now, why would I run off and leave the most beautiful woman in the world, alone."

I feel myself blushing, "That sounds like game."

"Baby, I don't play games. I know what I want and eventually, I'm going to have it." I hope you like the flowers. The lady at the front desk allowed me to pick them from the garden."

"I love them! They are beautiful! I've never gotten flowers before!"

"Wait, never? A man has never given you flowers?" Brian asked with a surprised look on his face.

"It's true, before today, I've never gotten flowers from a man," I said and held my head down realizing how sad that must have sounded. Here I am in my thirties and I've never even received flowers before. Damn, I guess that as worse as being a forty-year-old virgin.

Brian walked to me and sat on the bed near me. He kissed me on my lips and neck and put his finger under my chin and lifted my face up to meet his.

"Baby, you don't ever have to hold your head down around me. You have nothing to be ashamed of. I'm sorry those men couldn't see you true worth, but trust me. I see it. I love it and I want it. So, if you like flowers, I can't promise I'll bring them every day, but I'll send you flowers every week just to see that beautiful smile on your face."

Tears filled my eyes. Since I was young, I let people use me and take advantage of me. After my uncle raped me, I didn't feel worthy of anybody or anything. I allowed boys to use me because it made me feel good about myself. It made me feel wanted but as soon as it was over the feeling would return, so I was always on the move to get that feeling back. It was like chasing that very first high and sad to say, I never found it because I never experienced it. My uncle stole everything away from me and I've been searching all my life to find it.

I thought having children would have changed my way of thinking and make me happier, but I couldn't even do that right. I had three children by three married men, none who are in their child's life. Sure they pay child support, but it has never been the same and I feel so bad that my kids don't have their father in their lives.

Brian must have saw the tears in my eyes and kissed me and pulled me to him. Its okay, Rachel. I'm not going anywhere except to go get your breakfast. Since the breakfast was delivered early, I knew it was going to be cold by the time you woke up, so I told the kitchen staff to put your plate up until you were awake. I'll go get your food and get you some coffee from downstairs. Be right back!"

I got up and when to the bathroom and washed the dried tears from my face. I've never felt so loved. I've never spent this much time with a man without having sex or without him getting what he wanted and leaving me. Brian seems too good to be true. My heart is trying to accept his love without overthinking it, but my mind is reminding me of how many times, I opened my heart, only to get another hole placed in it. Before I could just analyze everything in my head, Brian was back with breakfast.

"Go ahead and eat and I'll be right back, I promise," Brian said with a slight smirk that looked like he was up to something.

By the time, I finished eating, Brian still wasn't back, so I took a quick shower and changed clothes. I put on some leggings and a t-shirt, I had gotten from Wal-Mart. As I was packing up my things before the 12:00 check-out, Brian walked in, smiling.

"What are you smiling about?" I asked.

"You'll see. First I need to get our things in the car before check-out time and then I have a surprise for you!"

Brian took all the bags to the car and returned. "Are you ready to go?"

"Yes, I'm ready!"

When we walked outside, there was two rental bicycles parked out front. I remember seeing the bikes at a shop not too far from the inn, when we were walking to the beach yesterday.

"I hope you can ride a bike!" Brian said to me.

"Yes, I can ride a bike. You know what they say, once you learn, you never forget."

"Cool, so guess what we are doing?" We are going to ride bikes around the island and sightsee, take pictures and selfies, and just act like kids before going back home to reality. How does that sound?"

"That sounds wonderful, Brian. Thank you for this. For everything. You have truly been here for me, through this entire ordeal and I am forever grateful for having you in my life."

I felt like a child riding the bicycles with Brian throughout town. Flashbacks of my life with my grandmother filled my head. I remember me and the girls riding our bikes together cutting blocks and racing. Seems like an eternity ago. Sharon, Tammie, Persia, and I were tighter that quadruplets. They were the sisters that I never had and I treated them all like crap.

When I get back home, I got to make amends and get everyone back together again. We rode the bikes for about an hour and a half, before stopping at one of the local shops for lunch. After eating lunch, we returned the bike rentals, checked out the inn and headed back to our real lives. Brian had to go back to face Nicole and I had to go and really face the issue that my baby boys are gone.

The ride home was a quiet one. Reality was settling in and Brian seemed occupied. I know people were going to think that I was making another big mistake, but at this point in my life. I'm done worrying about what people would think.

I called Sharon and let her know that I was on my way home and I spoke briefly with my kids. They all seemed to be in good spirits. Brian called Chico to see if Nicole was still in jail, but was surprised to know that she was out on bail. He downplayed the conversation, but I could tell that he was pissed and wondering who bailed her out and why the hell she hadn't called him.

I leaned over in my seat and kissed him on the neck and cheek.

"Thanks for everything, Brian. You didn't have to be her for me, but you were and that means a lot to me! I had a great time and you've helped me put a lot into perspective."

"You don't have to thank me, Rachel. Everything happens for a reason. Our paths were destined to cross for whatever reason, God wanted me here at this moment with you. I know it sounds crazy and it may even sound like game, but I believe in fate. If you tell anyone else I said that, I will deny it, but seriously, this is no accident," he said while grabbing my hand and kissing it.

"Brian, I'm scared. I've never been in a real relationship. I'm not sure if I even know how to be in a relationship. All I know is that I want to be in a real relationship. I want to know what it feels like to go to sleep with YOUR man and to wake up next to him. I want to get flowers just because and do things publicly like people in relationships do. Most of all, I want to fall in love and actually have that person love me back. I've wasted so many years and so much of my time on losers and thugs just because I didn't love myself enough to say I deserve better, but one thing I learned from Mikele and Mikye's death is that life is too short to live unhappily. So, I'm step out on fate and see where this goes. I like you, Brian and I see myself falling for a guy like you, but we cannot cross that bridge until you settle things with your wife. I know how bad secrets can destroy friendships and relationships. So, if it's really over, let her know. You owe her that much and yes she could have told you that she wasn't happy instead of cheating, but now is the time for you to be the bigger person and let her know how you truly feel."

"I like you too, Rachel. Although, it feels more like I'm falling in love with you. I know it's way too soon to be saying something like that, but I want to always be honest with you. I don't want any secrets between us."

"Okay, Brian. No secrets."

We rode the rest of the way, listening to the radio. We arrived at Sharon's house around six o' clock in the evening. The yard was filled with cars, so I could tell it was a lot of people over. I really didn't expect to be around a lot of people so soon, but I would eventually have to be around them, so I might as well start now.

Brian parked and helped me with my bags. As soon as I walked in the door, all three of my children ran to me and hugged me tight. Besides being with Brian, my kids made me feel so much better. Just seeing them smile did wonders for my heart.

As we entered the house, I saw Tammie, Sharon, and Persia in the kitchen. Mike, Mont, and Derek was in the den area, playing pool and Terrell said the rest of the children were downstairs playing the game.

I went into the kitchen and Sharon walked over and hugged me.

"Sharon, this is Brian," I said.

"Hi, Sharon. Nice to meet you," Brian said nervously.

Persia came over and hugged me as well and introduced herself to Brian. Tammie looked like she wanted to come over, but she didn't.

"Oh, so I can't get a hug Tamm?" I said laughing.

A smile crept on her face, as she walked over and hugged me.

"We good, Tamm. I'm not mad at you. I forgive you and I hope you can forgive me," I whispered in her ear.

"I forgive you," she muttered back.

She introduced herself to Brian and well. I must admit, it felt weird us all being together again, but it also felt like we could finally get pass what happened.

"Let's go to the den with the guys, that's where the bar is anyway, and I definitely can use a drink," Sharon said while sneaking a peek at Brian.

I'm sure she felt uncomfortable with him being there. Hell, I felt uncomfortable for her and I felt bad for Brian. I'm sure it wasn't easy for him to be here at the house of his wife's girlfriend.

On the way to the den, I pulled him to the side. "Are you okay?"

"Yes, I'm okay," he responded and kissed me.

I looked around to see who was watching us, but everyone else had went ahead into the den. I kissed Brian and we got lost in each other kisses, until we heard glass shuttering outside. We ran to the front door as Sharon and the others emerged from the den.

"Not this again!" Mont said.

When we got outside, we saw Nicole beating up Brian's car. She was bursting windows and making dents all over his car with a baseball bat. Persia took out her phone and started recording while Brian ran towards Nicole yelling at her to stop. Nicole didn't stop. She took out a knife and started putting all four of Brian's tires on flat.

"I see you and your little hoe made it back safe and sound! I hope you had a good trip, bitch!" she yelled at Brian, but looking directly at me when she said *Bitch.*

"Your issue is with your husband, not me! I don't owe you shit! So you best direct your anger at him!" I yelled at Nicole.

"Just be quiet, Rachel." Sharon called the police on her phone. Brian was still yelling at her to stop, while Mont and Derek just laughed and watched everything play out. Tammie and Persia was also quiet, but they looked like they were ready to attack if Nicole came at them.

"Fuck you, Bitch! I bet you won't bring your ass off that porch!" Nicole screamed at me.

"That's probably what you want to do, but sorry I don't play for your team. I'm team Brian over here!" I said. I really didn't try to be petty, but it was like all my built up anger and frustrated was slowly escaping and this bitch was about to get it.

"RACHEL! JUST LET IT GO!" Tammie said to me.

"Oh, so you a funny hoe, too? OKAY!" Nicole said and started walking towards the porch with the bat still in her hand, but I wasn't about to back down. I started walking down the steps, but Tammie and Sharon pushed me into the house and told me to stay there.

In the house, I looked out the window and I saw Brian walking towards Nicole. Once Brian got within a few feet of Nicole and the car, she swung the bat at him barely missing him. Brian jumped back and yelled, "You hit me with that bat and I promise, I will hit you back."

"Fuck you! Hit me, then! Hit me! You over here with that bitch and you want to hit me because you got caught!" Nicole screamed while still walking towards Brian.

"Wait! Are you serious right now? Caught doing what? Being over YOUR GIRLFRIEND house? Is that why you mad, because I'm allowed over here and you're not!" When he said that, it pissed her off big time and she started walking faster towards him. This time Brian didn't move and when she lifted the bat to swing at him. He grabbed her arm making her drop the bat. He pulled both of her arms behind her back as if she was under arrest and held her like that until the police came.

The police came and luckily it was Brian's friend Chico and his partner, Dave. Chico put Nicole in handcuffs and put her in the police car. Dave started getting statements from me and everyone else, while Chico took pictures of Brian's damaged car. After the police left, everyone went back inside except Brian and me. He called his insurance company to file a claim and get his car towed from Sharon's house.

"I'm going to go home while Nicole is in jail and pack my things and put them in storage. When I am done. I want to spend some time with you, if that possible," Brian said to me, while I sat outside with him until the tow truck came.

"It will have to be late, I want to spend some time with my kids and just take a few moments to just absorb everything and decided where to go from here," I responded.

"I understand that!" Brian said and put his arms around my shoulders as we sat on the steps waiting on the tow truck.

21

SHARON

I never saw this side of Nicole before yesterday. I knew she was bossy, but her take charge attitude is what initially drew me to her. I never in a million years would have thought she was this crazy, deranged, jealous, selfish, self-centered person that she has revealed herself to be in the last two days. I'm glad I found out before I proposed to her, but on the inside, I'm wondering how I was so blind that I didn't even see that this was how she really is. She had me fooled. The way I loved her, I didn't think I could love anyone like that, but it was all a lie.

After Nicole's meltdown with Brian, the mood of the house took a drastic turn. Everybody was quiet, but the noises from the herd of elephants in the room could be heard and felt miles away.

Even though we were all together, we've never been so far apart. Tammie and Mike were avoiding each other because of their pending divorce. Mike was trying to reach out to Rachel, but she was evading him. Tammie and Rachel made amends, but Tammie were still quite nervous being in the same room as her. Rachel must have felt the same way, because she went upstairs to lie down.

Persia kept ignoring Derek, who was constantly trying to talk to her. And since Mont and I already talked, there was no need for us to avoid each other.

Mont and I decided to go get dinner, since I really didn't feel like cooking. We ended up going to KFC.

We ate in silence, while the kids ate downstairs in the Basement. Once again, the silence took over and after dinner, the guys retreated to the den to shoot pool and Persia started making mixed drinks.

I got the playing cards and the dominoes out of the kitchen drawer and went into the den with the guys.

"Who's ready for an ass-whooping? Choose your weapon, cards or dominoes?" I said and laughed.

"Sharon, you know you can't play dominoes. You lose every time!" Mike said.

"I been practicing, so come on let me beat you!"

"Ok, I'm in! Let's do it!" Mike replied.

"Me, too," said Mont.

"I want to play Spades," Derek said.

"Well, it's not enough of us to play dominoes and spades so we play one game of dominoes, then one game of spades and alternate," I responded to Derek.

"Ok, let's go play then as they all got up and followed me into the kitchen."

"Okay, Persia, we going to need a lot more mixed drinks. First game of Dominoes, is going to be me, Mont, Mike, and Tammie. Derek you can help Persia with the mixed drinks. I have tequila in the fridge if you guys prefer shots over the margaritas. We can start in a minute, I'm going to take Rachel some food and check on her."

As I started up the stairs to check on Rachel, I said a quick prayer to God, to please not let anyone kill each other. My plan was to partner the people together that had issues to work out. So far it seemed to be working. Even if only for a minute, we were all communicating among each other again.

"Rachel, are you okay?" I asked walking into the room.

"Yea, I'm okay. Just trying to get a little rest," Rachel replied.

"Ok, well I'll let you rest but I brought you something to eat and a soda. I'm put it on the dresser for you. Let me know if you need anything else."

"Well, there is one more thing. I don't want to intrude, but can I stay here a few days? I can't bear to go home right now," Rachel said sorrowfully.

"Girl, you free to stay here as long as it take. Just get you some rest and we will talk about this later," I said.

I gave her a hug and went back downstairs so Mont and I could beat Tammie and Mike in dominoes. The first thing, I noticed was Persia and Derek missing from the kitchen. I didn't go looking for them, I'm just glad that they were at least talking through whatever they were dealing with.

The game started and despite their pending divorce Tammie and Mike actually came together as a team and won the game. Although they didn't win by much, it was great seeing them talking again.

Just as we were about to start another game, Persia and Derek came in and got another margarita. All of a sudden, we heard Rachel scream out. We rushed up the stairs and burst in the bedroom and found Rachel in the middle of the bed balled up in fetal position. She appeared to be in a daze, but when I called her name, she looked confused.

"What's everybody doing in here?"

"We heard you scream and came to see what was wrong," I told her.

"I was screaming? I must have had a bad dream or something. I can't remember. I'm okay, though. Sorry I scared you guys."

Everybody went back downstairs except me. I stayed behind to make sure Rachel was really okay. I could tell that she did remember her dream, but she just didn't want me to worry us.

"Are you sure you okay, Rachel?"

"I'm okay, Sharon. You don't have to worry about it. I'm fine and I promise I'm not going to do anything stupid," she said.

"Well, I'm here if you want to talk. You don't have to deal with this alone. Despite everything between us and the people downstairs, we all love you Rachel and we all care," I said hugging her.

Her phone started ringing interrupting our hug.

"Hey, Brian!" Rachel said into the phone.

I left and went back downstairs. Derek, Persia, Mike and Tammie were starting a game of dominoes. I went down to the basement to check on the children and they all were knocked out sleep. When I came back upstairs, Mont had made a fresh batch of margaritas and Tammie was already on her second drink from the new batch. Tammie never could handle her liquor, so it was just a matter of time before things got out of hand.

"Okay, Tammie that's enough for you. I'm have to be like the bartender and cut you off because you have reached your limit!" I said to Tammie in a stern tone, so she would know that I was serious.

"Girl please, I'm grown. I know my limit and right now I'm nowhere near it!" Tammie replied in an aggressive tone.

"Tammie, just slow down. You have been drinking a lot tonight," Mike said passively

"Whatever, you don't get to tell me what to do anymore remember Mike? You lost that privilege weeks again, remember?"

"Tammie, don't do this. Now is not the time nor the place," I said.

"I'm sorry Sharon. Tammie, I apologize. You right. I can't tell you what to do anymore!" Mike said.

"Tammie, why did you do that?" I asked her.

"Do what? We are getting a divorce, so it's no point in pretending."

"Nobody asked you to pretend, Tammie!" Persia spoke up. "You didn't have to handle things like that. Derek and I aren't together either, but you don't see us making a big deal about anything. Hell, Mont and Sharon aren't together either, but nobody made a scene, but you! Regardless of what goes on between you and Mike, you are going to always be connected because of your children, same as Derek and Persia, same as Mont and I, same as Mike and....." I stopped after realizing I had gone too far, but it was too late.

Tammie knew what I was about to say and finished the sentence for me.

"Mike and Rachel? Is that what you were going to say? Yes, I know. Rachel and Mike will always be connected! Although, there are no kids anymore to---"

A plate hit the floor before Tammie could finish. Rachel had come downstairs and walked in on Tammie talking.

I rushed to Rachel, who was frozen in place, but the tears flowed freely down her face. She was hurt and you can tell that hearing Tammie say that about her boys hurt her to her soul. I tried to get Rachel to go back upstairs with me, but she didn't move. I heard Persia telling Tammie that she was wrong and she shouldn't have said that.

Rachel wiped her eyes and started walking towards Tammie. Tammie saw Rachel coming and hopped up in a defensive stance.

"I'm not going to fight you, Tammie! Fighting you is not going to bring my boys back nor is it going to change who their father is. You want to blame me for your marriage not working, but where is your accountability. Mike checked out of your marriage long before I ever fucked him. It's not my fault you could satisfy him. Maybe if you had took the time to actually talk to him instead psychoanalyzing him and every argument, your marriage probably could have worked!"

Tears filled Tammie eyes and she looked as if she wanted to punch Rachel, but instead she fell back into her chair and cried. Rachel turned around and went back upstairs.

"Persia, take Tammie home, please. The kids can stay here," I said.

"Sure, Sharon, but I'm going to go on home after I drop Tammie off, I'll be over in the morning to get the kids."

"Tammie, you were wrong. Those babies had nothing to do with this and as a mother, how could you say something like that? Thanks guys for everything. I'll come get the kids in the morning. Good night," Mike said as he grabbed his keys and prepared to left.

"I'm about to leave too. Sharon, I'll talk to you tomorrow. Good night, guys." Mont said.

"Me too. Thanks for everything Sharon. I'll be back in the morning to see the kids before I head back out to Nashville," Derek stated.

Mike, Mont, and Derek, all left out together. They stood outside talking near their cars before saying goodbye and going their separate ways.

Persia left to take Tammie home and I went upstairs to check on Rachel. I found her sitting on the floor crying. She was doing one of those hyperventilate-type cries. I couldn't tell if she was having a panic attack or if she just crying real hard. I ran back down stairs and got one of the brown lunch bags.

"Here breathe into the bag, Rachel."

She did as I told her and her breathing regulated a little but she continued to cry hysterically. I didn't talk, I just let her cry and get everything out. At times, I cried with her. After about an hour, she went from hyperventilate-crying to weeping and silent tears.

She got up from the floor and began to get ready for bed when her phone started to ring. I'm sure it was Brian again, so I told her good night and went to my own room to go to bed. A few moments passed and I heard Rachel run down the stairs and out the door. I went downstairs, into the kitchen, and looked out the window to see what Rachel was doing. She was outside with Brian, so I went back upstairs and got ready for bed.

TAMMIE

Perhaps, I was drunk or maybe it just needed to be said. Whatever it was, I'm sorry I hurt Rachel, but all the pain and heartache she caused me didn't just go away because her babies died. I'm sorry the twins died but I'm tired of acting like everything is good.

I tried forgiving Rachel and I know she tried to forgive me but no matter how hard we tried, neither one of us could ever forget the betrayal and pain, we caused each other. I know she still blames me for the twins' death and I blame her for the issues in my marriage. It may not have been entirely her fault, but she shouldn't have been the person, he unloaded our marital problems on. Even if he tried, she should have been strong enough to tell him NO!

I did have too much to drink and Persia had to take me home. I expected her to lecture me about what I did to Rachel, but she didn't say a word. The entire ride home was filled with silence. Persia dropped me off and didn't say goodbye or even wait until I made it inside the house before she left.

Everything changes. Change is necessary for growth and I just feel like in order for me to grow pass everything between Mike and Rachel, I had to take myself out of the equation and all things associated with it.

PERSIA

Tammie was always the glue that held us together, but now she was the one that destroyed what was left of us. As a psychiatrist, she had to know that what she said to Rachel would be devastating. For that brief moment, it seemed as if she really wanted to hurt Rachel. It was as if she had been waiting on an opportunity to get revenge. My momma always said *there are three people that tell the truth: babies, drunk people, and old people.* Even though Tammie was drunk, everything she said was something that she always wanted to say, but lacked the courage.

I didn't say anything to her on the drive to her house. I put her out and left. My mind was too full and plus I was mad at her for being so insensitive to Rachel. She said some really hurtful things and as a mother, I just don't see how she could say things like that to another mother. We've been friends since we were little, so I'm sure eventually we would be close again.

Derek and I managed to talk briefly before all hell broke loose and although we were going our separate ways, surprisingly we came to an understanding that being apart was the best thing for us to grow. He was leaving to go back to Nashville in the morning. He even told me that he was with Taylor.

We talked about his sexuality and he assured me that he wasn't gay and that he has never had sex with a man. He explained that Taylor had the gender reassignment surgery at age 18 and that she was a woman that just happen to be born a man.

I didn't bother getting into the specifics with him because frankly, it was no longer my business what he did. As long as he continued to be a father to his kids, I had nothing to do with his relationships.

I think we tried to force something to be that we lost a long time ago and we stayed for the kids hoping that being parents would help us fall back in love again, but we were wrong. He found in Taylor what was missing from our marriage and I found it in Deniji.

Although, I hate how things played out between us, for the sake of our kids, I'm glad that we can at least be civilized with each other for the sake of our kids.

I didn't feel like going home alone, so I called Deniji. He answered on the fourth or fifth ring.

"Hey hun, I can't sleep and I don't want to go home. Can I come over?"

"Sure, baby! I'll leave the door unlock for you. See you when you get here," Deniji said sleepily.

I arrived at Deniji's house. I went in, locked the door, and crawled in bed next to him. I kissed him on the cheeks and neck before I laid my head on his chest and listened to the rhythm of his heartbeat. Deniji kissed me on the forehead and said, "I love you!" As much as I was afraid to fall in love again, I couldn't fight the fact that I had fallen for Deniji and that I loved him too.

"I love you too!" I whispered.

MIKE

These last few weeks have been the hardest days of my life. I lost my twin boys, Tammie filed for divorce, and I've been living out of a hotel until I find me a more permanent place. Spending all that time with Rachel, helped me realized that deep down, I really did have feelings for her, but Rachel felt that our affair is the reason that the twins got sick and died. That somehow, God was punishing us for our affair by taking our children.

I understand how she could feel like that and for a minute, I thought the same time too. I know God don't make mistakes and he has a plan for everything. Even though, their time here on this earth was short and my time with them was even shorter, my heart still aches from losing them. They were my children and for some reason, everybody act as if I'm not grieving or sad about the kids' death. I guess you have to be crying, falling out, breaking things, or cursing for people to understand that you are in fact grieving.

Everybody grieves differently and because Rachel was so vulnerable, I had to step up and be there for her, as well as for my kids and her kids because they lost their brothers and Tammie felt that I was including everyone but her. The fact that she never got over me getting Rachel pregnant and then having to watch me be at the hospital every day was too much for her.

I knew it was coming. Even before Rachel and I started messing around, my marriage to Tammie was strained. She became more of a psychiatrist than my wife. Every argument turned into a therapy session. There was no communication whatsoever. We would talk, but that's all it was talking. She wasn't listening and because of her job, she felt that she was always right and I was always wrong. So, being in a relationship where nothing you do is right or good enough, it made sense to seek that acceptance elsewhere. I hate that I sought that acceptance in Rachel, but it's too late for that now. All I can do now, is move on and after the events tonight, I am ready for the new start.

I still don't understand how Tammie could be so cruel to Rachel. She basically stated that she's glad the twins are death. As a mother, I just don't see how she could say that to another mother, when she gets worried if our children bus is five minutes late.

Rachel was still having a hard time dealing with everything, but she don't want me around to comfort her, plus she has Brian now. I don't know Brian that well, but he seems to really be feeling Rachel. At first, I was a little upset seeing them together, but then I realized that she and I would never be together because of how we started. The fact that we started out as a fling, no one would take us seriously and the stigma of me being with my ex-wife best friend, would never go away. So, there is nothing left to do but embrace this newfound singlehood, take things slow and see what happens.

DEREK

Persia and I are done, but I feel good knowing that after our little talk, we are going to do our best to co-parent like reasonable adults. It feels greats knowing that there are no more secrets between us. Actually it seems like we get along better apart than we ever did together. Taylor has been blowing my phone up, but I told her it's way too soon to bring her around and conduct introductions. She was upset that I wouldn't allow her to be with me the last few days, but I couldn't disrespect my family like that and upset everyone especially doing this hard time.

I think Taylor thought that by me being around Persia and my kids, that I would leave her and go back to my family. I assured her that I wasn't going anywhere, but that I had to be there for my family.

The funeral and the days following it was kind of rough, but somehow Persia and I managed without killing each other. We had some tense moments, where it started sinking in that this time, it was really over, but we talked about it and came to an understanding because when it's all said and done, we still have two children to raise.

I told her that I was moving to Nashville and that Taylor and I was going to be a couple. Although, I could see that she had some feelings about me being with Taylor, she didn't say anything. I told her that I would come back to Georgia two weekends a month to see the kids and spend time with them. I informed her that as always I would continue to take care of our children.

We worked out the other arrangements about our children and she even told me that she was pursuing a relationship with Deniji, the African guy that I got into a fight with. Honestly, I would have felt better if she had chosen Antwan, because at least I know him. I don't know anything about Deniji, except that he is African and Persia likes him a lot.

I wished her well as she did me. Even though our marriage was not official, walking away from someone you spent so many years with was hard, but when you truly love someone, you don't

239

want to hold on to them just to keep them from someone else. You learn to let them go and find the love that they so deserve from someone else, especially after you realize you cannot give them the very thing that they need! Letting go is hard but staying together when there is nothing else is even harder.

No matter what the future holds for us both, the bond we have will always be there because she was my high school sweetheart and she is the mother of my children and Taylor or anyone else can ever come between that.

MONT

Being with my family these last few days has made me realize just how much I want my family back. Waking up and being able to see my wife, well ex-wife, and walk down the hall and see my kids fast asleep in their beds or being able to watch a movie with them or take them out at any time felt wonderful.

I can't lie and say that I love women and only women because that would be a lie, but Sharon is the only woman I have ever truly loved. I wish I could change what happened between us, but I can't. Our marriage ended because I was not only in love with her, but I thought I was in love with my best friend/boyfriend Marcus. Marcus and I were reckless and got caught up in our indiscretions.

That's a horrible way for anyone to find out that there husband is bisexual and that day has always haunted me. Not because of the picture she took, but because that was the day I saw hatred in her eyes and that was the day that I realized that I truly hurt the mother of my children.

Sharon eventually forgave me, but up until a few months back, our relationship was really strained. I avoided her and missed out on very important times and memories with my children because I was ashamed.

We eventually found a common ground and was acting getting into the swing of co-parenting when we messed up and slept together stirring up old feelings and lots of confusion. If it meant living a lie, I was willing to do that as long as I got to wake up to her and my children, but Sharon wasn't going for it. She wanted to live her life happy and without secret and lies.

The truth was Sharon was gay and she embraced who she was. She didn't care what society thought of her. I admired her strength and maybe one day, I, too, could be as bold and strong as she is.

Although there was a time when I wasn't there for my family, I thanked her for giving me another chance. Regardless of it all, we agreed to be there for each other and to continue to be great parents to our children.

22

BRIAN

On the ride home following Nicole's fight, I was still in disbelief. I can't believe Nicole came over Sharon's house cutting up again. Then she had the nerves to pretend as if I hurt her so bad when her ass is the one that has been cheating all along. It took everything in me not to whoop her ass. All the years, I damned near begged her to start a family and she knew all along that she was gay and never wanted to have children. That's the part that hurts the most, because she knew I wanted children.

Whoever got her out of jail the first time, better get her out this time as well, but I am not going to bail her out. The cars are in both of our names, so I know insurance is not going to fix the car, she damaged. Since she vandalized it, I'm going to make sure that is the car she gets in the divorce.

I pulled into the garage and went into the house, stopping in the kitchen long enough to get me a drink. It's crazy how I was so happy just hours earlier and it only took Nicole about thirty minutes to kill my vibe.

I'm really feeling Rachel and I truly enjoyed spending time with her. I know she is dealing with a lot, so I'm back off and give her some time to herself. Nicole has already shown that she is going to make things difficult and I don't want to bring Rachel and her kids into my mess. I just hope that Rachel hasn't moved on by the time this divorce is done.

I started packing my things when there was a knock at the door. It was Chico. He wanted to see if I was okay and to let me know that some woman bailed Nicole out of jail. He decided to stay a while since he was off duty and of course, he wanted me to hit the strip club with him. He helped me pack my things and since it was too late to get a storage, he let me put my things in his garage until I could get a storage. He even offered to let me stay with him until I decided what I wanted to do about the situation with Nicole. I called and checked on Rachel and she seemed to be doing okay.

After moving, we got dressed and went to the strip club. Of course, Chico quickly settled into his same old routine and Kandi did her striptease while mainly focusing on Chico. Watching the interactions between them two, reassures me that you can't help who you fall in love with and Chico had no problem admitting that he *was in love with a stripper.* I think the two were secretly dating, but Chico would not confirm.

As the night, turned into early morning, I couldn't stop thinking about Rachel. I wanted to call and talk to her, but decided to see her in person instead. Since Nicole vandalized the car I used, I drove the car she was using when she got arrested. I told Chico I was leaving and he assured me, he had a way home.

When I got close to Sharon's house, I called Rachel. I was surprised she was up.

"Hey, baby! I just wanted to check on you. I hope I didn't wake you. I just couldn't go to sleep without hearing your voice!" I said in my sexiest voice.

"Aww! That's sweet! No you didn't wake me. Actually I was just getting ready for bed," she replied.

"Oh okay, it's great hearing your voice. I wish I could see you right now, I bet you looking sexy."

"Well, I'm not looking all sexy as you think I am, but I'm up if you wanted to stop by," Rachel stated.

"Glad you said that cause I'm about to pull up now!"

"WHAT?! How you knew I was up?"

"I didn't know. I was just hoping that you were, The stars aligned, fate stepped in, and made it possible! I'm outside!"

Rachel came out with her hair bonnet on, a white A-shirt, and some black cheerleader shorts with white strips on the side, and flip flops. As excited as I was to see her, it seemed that she was equally excited to see me because she ran straight into my arms and hugged me tight.

Looking up at the sky, it seemed that the stars really did align to make this moment happen. A shooting star streaked across the sky. I closed my eyes and made a wish.

"Being here with you feels so right even though it is so wrong! I mean you belong to someone else, and I wish you were mines!" Rachel said sincerely.

"Rachel, my marriage was over before I even met you. I just refused to see it. I ignored the signs and tried my best to make it work, but I realized I was the only one trying and Nicole's affair with your friend confirmed that. I want you in my life, but I don't want to rush you. We can go as slow as you want, but just know I am going to do this right. I moved out and I'm staying with Chico until I find my own place. Tomorrow, I'm going to file for divorce and when you are ready to make us official, I'll be waiting!" I said to her with a smile and kissed her passionately and deeply.

Rachel broke the kiss and said, "I'm not trying to be with somebody else's husband, again. I'm done being the side chick. So, once you have your affairs in order, maybe we can see where things goes but for now, we are only friends."

"Well, in order to be in a relationship, you have to be good friends, first. So, I'll say we are on the right track and you'll be mines in no time!" I stated assertively.

We sat down on the steps like we had did earlier and watched the stars and talked. I can't remember everything we talked about, but I do know that I was enjoying every moment. I don't know what the future holds for me and Rachel, but I'm ready for the ride.

23

RACHEL

Three months later....

I still can't believe that Brian and I are engaged.

Every woman has fantasized about the day her man proposes to her and what her wedding will be like. Being the side chick for so long, I gave up looking for a man to propose to me or marry me. Brian changed all of that.

I didn't look for him. I didn't scheme to win his love and I didn't have sex to get his love nor to keep it. He actually loves me for me and that's the best feelings in the world. Not only me, but he loves my children as if they are his.

Sometimes, I watch how his face light up when they enter a room or when he is conversing with one of them, I can see how much he enjoys being around them and vice versa. Brian's unconditional love helped me tear down years of low self-esteem and trust issues.

Honestly, I never thought I could never be this happy again, especially after losing the twins. With the luck I've had, I want to say Brian is the perfect guy, but there is no such thing, but I do believe in soul mates and if soul mates are real, then Brian is my soul mate. He gets me on so many levels. His proposal was so unexpected, but so unforgettable.

The day Brian proposed, I was in my room, doubled up in pain from cramps, feeling all emotional watching *Silver Lining*. Bradley Cooper and Jennifer Lawrence were awesome in that movie. I was at my favorite part where she finally reads the letter that he wrote her when Brian walked in with gift bags.

"Turn this off for a minute baby, I got something for you!" he says to me.

Seeing all the bags, I got excited. He walked over to me and put the bags on the bed and kissed me.

I muted the T.V. and he sat down by me on the bed.

"There are four parts to this. So, here is part one," he states and hands me a purple bag with light purple and while tissue paper hanging out of the top of the bag.

I wasn't expecting any gifts because it wasn't my birthday or any type of holiday so to be getting *I thought of you today* gifts made my heart smile. I opened the bag and pulled out two stacks of romance DVDS.

He had *Love Jones, Jason's Lyric, Love and Basketball, How Stella Got Her Groove Back, Paris Blue, Brown Sugar, The Best Man, Mahogany, Boomerang, Deliver Us from Eva, Poetic Justice, Why Did I Get Married?, and Two Can Play that Game.*

By the time, I reached the last DVD, I was in tears. Brian had purchased all of my favorite Romance movies. Nobody has ever done anything like that for me.

Brian reached over and wiped my eyes, "Don't cry, baby! You still have three more parts," and he handed me the second bag.

This bag was hot pink with light pink and white tissue paper hanging out of the top. This bag was also kind of heavy. I reached in the bag and pulled out books. Lots and lots of books! He had titles by Terry McMillian, Zane, Eric Jerome Dickey, Omar Tyree, Nicholas Spark, KiKi Swanson, Wahilda Clark, Jessica Watkins, and Niyah Moore.

Again the waterworks started and I was speechless. Brian pulled me to him, wiped my face and kissed where the tears had been.

"There's two more parts, so you have to save some tears for those," he said as he handed me the final bag.

This bag was red with white tissue paper hanging out of the top of the bag. This bag was not as heavy as the other. I opened the bag and pulled out a big bag of Hot Cheetos chips, a pack of chocolate chip cookies, a pack of lemon cookies, a Snickers, a Twix, a Turtles Candy bar, a Milky Way, and Talenti caramel cookie crunch gelato, chocolate chip cookie dough gelato, and double dark chocolate.

So, not only did he get my favorite movies and books, he also made me a Period Care Package. The tears were welding up again. "Thank you so much Brian!" I said as I reached over to give him a hug and a kiss.

"You're welcome, baby but there is still one more part." He got up and put his phone in the speaker dock on the nightstand.

Marry Me by Jason Derulo started playing. When he turned around his button up shirt was unbuttoned exposing a black t-shirt underneath that read, *MARRY ME?* My heart skipped a beat and no longer able to hold the tears, they flowed down my face like a faucet.

Brian started singing along to the song as he walked over to me and kneeled down in front of me. I caught snips and pieces of Brian singing before, but I didn't know that he could really sing because he would always stop when he noticed me listening to him.

Brian serenaded me until the song ended and pulled a ring box from his pocket and opened it exposing a princess cut engagement ring.

"Rachel, I want to be the first thing you see in the mornings and the last thing you see at night. I want to be the one that wipe your tears when you watch your favorite romance movies. I want to be the one to give the happily ever after that you read about in books. I want to be your husband. Will you make me the happiest man in the world and be my wife?" he asked.

"YES!!! A THOUSAND TIMES, YES!!! I said as I kneeled down on the floor with him.

We kissed for what seemed like minutes before finally breaking apart.

"Okay, which movie you want to watch first? Or do you want to read for a while?

"Let's watch *Love Jones*!" I replied and we laid in bed all day eating junk food and watching movies.

*****

"Awww, Rachel! I'm so happy for you. You deserve this. Maybe one day, I will find my happiness," Sharon said.

"You will, Sharon. If I can find true love after finding so much wrong love and all the bad karma I've had, then surely you can find love as well. But I learned you don't have to chase love. When it's real you'll know. You won't have to look for it, because it will find you. You just have to be willing to accept it!"

"I guess you right, Rachel! Now come on let toast to your new beginnings!"

The waitress brought out our margaritas and Patron shots.

"Congratulations on your engagement, Rachel! I love you and I am the maid of honor or we go have issues!"

"Deal, but only if I'm the maid of honor at your wedding!"

"Well, I got to find *the one* first! Maybe I'll find me a wife or *SOMEBODY ELSE'S WIFE* will find me!" Sharon stated.

"You will be okay, Sharon. Your Prince Charming or Princess is coming," I stated.

"Well, we will see but he or she needs to hurry up! I'm getting impatient! Anyway, girl I'll talk to you later. I got some errands to run."

24

SHARON

I'm so happy Rachel finally got her happily ever after. She deserves it. She's been through so much in her life and to see her finally overcoming it all is wonderful! I thought I would be happily engaged by now, but Nicole turned out to be just another frog pretending to be a princess.

After leaving Rachel, I decided to finish up some errands and head home. When I got home, Mont was waiting for me in the driveway. He normally calls me before he comes over, so the fact that he didn't meant that this was serious. I wonder what caused him to pop up unannounced.

I hurry out of my car and walk over to Mont's car. He doesn't get out of the car. I knocked on the window and without even looking up, he motioned for me to get in. I walk around the car to get in the passenger's side. As soon as I sat down, I knew something was wrong.

"Sharon, why did you do it?" Mont asked me sternly and with anger.

"Do what, Mont? What happened and what is wrong with you?" I asked with concern.

"Don't play dumb, Sharon!" Mont replied.

"Mont, I don't know what the hell you talking about, so tell me what you think I did?" I stated with much attitude.

"I lost my job today. The entire board got an email from someone about me and Marcus and that picture you took years ago!" Mont yelled with tears in his eyes as he placed his Ipad on my lap. The Ipad had an open email with an image attached. I scrolled down to the picture and sure enough it was the picture that I took.

I didn't leak the picture but I definitely knew who did.

"Mont, I didn't do this. I would never do that. I've had that picture for years, if I wanted to hurt you, I would have done it when we were on bad terms. Why would I do that to you now, when you are just getting back in the kids' lives and things are going well between us?"

"If you didn't do it, then who else could have done it? Who else knows about the picture?" Mont asked.

"The only other person that saw that picture was...NICOLE! Shit, it had to be her. Damn! Mont, I'm sorry, but I had nothing to do with her sending that picture. Honestly! I'm sure she did this to get back at me, because I broke up with her. I hate you got caught up with this, but I'll take care of it! Just pull yourself together, Mont. You can stay here until you calm down because I don't want you to do something you would regret. I'll let the kids stay over Tammie tonight but I'm going to have to take them some changing clothes and stuff. Come on, let's go inside and figure all this out!"

I knew Nicole was mad, but I never thought she would do something like this to hurt me. What if that email goes viral and my kids have to deal with the backlash? It's one thing to be mad at me, but to do something that could possibly hurt my children was asking for trouble and that's exactly what she is going to get.

"Why don't you go upstairs and lay down for a while? I'm going to take the kids some clothes and stuff over Tammie's since they are spending the night. Once I return, we can sit down and try figure out our next step," I said to Mont.

"Okay, Sharon. Thanks for everything."

"No problem, Mont. We are family whether we are together or not," I said as I followed Mont up the stairs.

Mont went into the guest bedroom and closed the door. I went into my closet and grabbed my glock 9mm pistol and stuffed it into my purse and left. Nicole already proved herself to be a little cray-cray and I wasn't about to take any chances. As I got in my car, an eery feeling overcame me.

***

I parked two houses down from Nicole's house and got out and walked to the door. I was just about to knock but the door was already cracked opened. I took my gun out of my purse, turned the safety off, and slowly pulled the slide on top of the gun to load the bullet into the firing chamber, just like Mike showed me. I thank God for Mike, because he helped me out a lot with the man stuff after Mont and I first divorced.

I tiptoed into the house and as soon as I entered the living room area, my mouth hit the floor. Mont was standing in the living room, near the sofa with his glock 9mm pistol drawn on Nicole, who was balled up on the couch, too scared to move or talk. Even though, I had my gun drawn on her as well, the look on her face, almost made me feel sorry for her. Almost, but it passed really quick as the reason for my visit popped in my head.

Mont quickly looked at me and back to Nicole.

"If you yell, scream, or make any noise or movement, I will fucking kill you!" He said to Nicole aggressively.

"What the hell you doing here, Sharon?" he inquired.

"Apparently the same thing you are. I told you this is not just about you. Our kids could get caught up in this shit and I'm not about to let that shit pass!" I replied, while looking Sharon dead in her eyes. "Nobody is going to hurt my family, NO ONE!"

Nicole tried to say something, but Mont hit her in the face with his gun and she cried out in pain. She looked at me, as if she wanted me to stop Mont.

"You reap what you sow! You planted this seed and now it has come back to bite you in the ass. Honestly, Nicole I don't care what Mont does to you, because you deserve everything he decides to do to you, but before he starts on his plan for you. I'm tell you what I want you to do. I want you to sent another email to the board from that phony email address you created, explaining to them that the picture is fake and that you are sorry for sending it. You are going to explain that you are just a jilted lover who was mad at her ex-boyfriend and wanted to get revenge. Do you understand me?" I said to Nicole sternly.

With tears in her eyes, she shook her head yes. Mont looked at me, his eyes trying to have a conversation, but I ignored him. He may have thought this was about him, but it wasn't. This was about protecting my children and I would stop at nothing to do that.

"Take her over to the computer, so she can do what I told her. After that, she's all yours. You can do whatever you want to her, I don't care. I just want her out of my life!" I directed to Mont.

Mont followed Nicole to the computer desk just as she was about to sit down, she pulled the computer chair out really fast and hit Mont between the legs with the back of the chair and grabbed the keyboard. Before she could hit him with the keyboard, a gun went off and she fell to the floor.

TO BE CONTINUED...

SOMEBODY ELSE'S WIFE: SHARON'S STORY   coming soon

Sneak Peek

Illicit Lovers: Secrets of a Wife

MEET THE WIVES: PLEASURE & KIARA

Dear Diary,

Borrowed time seems to be the best time of my day. Although it's never long, it feels like forever. Crazy how stolen moments with Demetrius means more to me than the time I spend with my husband, Sy'Ere. How can something so wrong, feel so right? How can Demetrius have complete control over my body instead of my husband? The way my body reacts to Demetrius and how our bodies synch when we are near each other without so much as a word is amazing. A simple text from him, makes me wet.

I dare not say it is love, but merely lust, but whatever it is; I want

this feeling to last.

STOLEN MOMENTS

I heard a quote once that said, "Time is free but it is priceless. You can't own it, but you can use it. You can't keep it, but you can spend it. Once you've lost it, you can never get it back" so I learned to value my time by making each and every moment count, especially the stolen moments with you.

After being apart for so long, our time has finally come
I'm here with you right where I belong
There is no time to waste, for time is not on our side
It will all be over soon and then again you will be gone

Stolen moments are all we have
I'm not yours and you are not mines
But at this moment, it's our time.
After being apart for so long, we are finally together
You kiss me and I feel like I'm floating like the wind
guiding a feather
I fall to my knees in submission
I bow my head in silence
I raise my nates to greet you, they fall open like a broken heart
Your hands find them and push them back together
as if you trying mend my broken heart
For a minute, my heart is whole and locked again and only one have
the key
You insert your key into my lock to see if you are the one
The one that can unlock the secrets of my heart, the passion that
burns within me, the love that hides within....

Your key clicks in my lock, a perfect fit
Secrets are released
Memories are relived
Love fills the air all while we embrace this stolen moment

No words are needed, even though there's plenty to say
What's the point? As in your arms I lay, knowing that soon out time
will be done
You have to get back to your life and I have to get back to my mines
So my heart is locked again and
The key is hidden until the next time I need my broken heart
mended
I wish I could make this stolen moment last
But our time is done, until next time

So, we put back on our masks and get back to our lives all the while
reminiscing and waiting on our next stolen moment.......

Watching him sleep, I'm dreading waking him up so he can

go home to his wife. Yes, Demetrius is married. Sometimes I feel

bad about sleeping with somebody else's husband but then I think

about the women that are sleeping with my husband and I don't

care. I know that sounds harsh but it's the truth.

Sy'Ere works on the oil rig on the coast so he is only home a

couple days sometimes two weeks to a month at a time, which

makes it easier for Demetrius to come over most nights. My kids never see him here and I am very, very careful to never let them know I cheat on their father. As far as they know, I'm a great wife as well as I am a great mother.

The outlandish thing about it is that I know my husband Sy'Ere is doing the same thing while working out of town. My husband and I don't have a formal open marriage, but then again we kind of do. I know that he cheats on me and he suspects that I am cheating on him. We have a 'Don't ask, Don't tell policy. We take care of the household and kids and when one of us is out or going to be late, we simply don't ask questions. Again, crazy I know but it works for us. We actually don't argue anymore. Not sure if it's because of the policy or simply because I just ignore his ass. Either way, there is a little bit more peace in our house.

I'll write more later, it's time for me to wake up Demetrius so he can go home to his WIFE!

Kiara

Dear Diary,

Demetrius hasn't come home yet. Of course, he is with her. He is always there. Sometimes, I wish he would just leave me for her and then I could just move on with my life. Sitting here waiting on my husband to leave his mistress is not something that I planned to do in my marriage. If I had known this would be my life, I never would have gotten married.

I know Demetrius isn't in love with me anymore, but some part of him, just won't let me go. Truth be told, my love for him has diminished as well, but I'm not ready to let him go, or maybe I'm just afraid to let him go.

Now, things are escalating. He does not even care if I know he is out cheating. He is just sloppy with it or he doesn't care. He no longer tries to hide that he's with her. It's like he wants to hurt me

enough, so that I will finally say, fuck it and leave on my own. I

don't understand why he just won't leave me, if he doesn't love me

anymore.

YOU DON'T LOVE ME

You say you love me
But your actions say otherwise
If you don't love me, then let me be
Can't you see the tears my heart cries
You don't love me

I'm tired of an empty bed at night
I'm tired of the constant feeling of being alone
I'm tired of not having someone to hold me tight
I'm tired of a house that no longer feels like a home
That's not love and you don't love me

We are not even friends anymore
Neither are we lovers
Loving you has become a chore
I just don't see how this love can ever recover
There is no emotions
There is no passion
There is no affection
There is no love left
You don't love me, maybe you never did

But the sad truth is I don't love you either
I did love you but you caused that love to leave, yet I kept my true
feelings hid
You don't love me
And I don't love you

Everything's out in the open now
No more pretending
No more silence
No more games
The love has run out
The care is gone
My heart is locked and you no longer have the key
You don't love me and I don't love you so set me free!

My husband been lost interest in me. Not that I'm ugly or

anything like that. I guess married life just became too much for

him, so he had to find something or somebody to take his mind off

of the pressures of home.

I knew right away when he started cheating. He changed.

Of course, I made excuses for his behavior and convinced myself it

was all in my head and when denial stopped working, I did what

most women did and blamed myself!

I figured I had let myself go, so I tried everything I could to make myself presentable in his eyes. I redecorated our bedroom, updated my lingerie collection, invested in Bath & Body works and Victoria Secret products. I even tried spontaneous sex and being more creative with our sex life and nothing worked. I cried a couple of nights about it, wondering how we got to this point. Nothing I tried, worked. So at some point, I just stopped trying and it seems that once I stopped trying, he stopped caring and the disrespect began.

Like tonight, he is out late again. This makes the third time this week. I know he is with that bitch. He's always with her it seems. Shit, I'm starting to think she is the wife and I'm the side chick. Bet you wondering why I'm so nonchalant about it? Well, truth of the matter is that there nothing I can do about it. My husband and I been married ten years, but he has been having an affair with her for eight years.

I try not to say her name out loud. To me she is simply

HER, THE SIDE BITCH, THE HOME WRECKER, THE SLUT,

WHORE, etc., although I know her government. Her name is

Pleasure Johnson. I'm not go hate and say she ugly and ain't shit

because I'd be lying. The bitch is cute or whatever a little short

maybe about 5'5, dark skinned, thick, curvy girl. She wears her hair

natural, and she doesn't wear much makeup. She works at the

college as an admission clerk. Crazy thing is the bitch is married

herself, but her husband works out of town a lot, so he's rarely

home. I wonder do he know his wife is fucking around on him. Shit,

I'm sure he does, but he may be like me and just realize it ain't

nothing he can do to stop her, especially if he is barely at home.

It's almost four a.m. and Demetrius still hasn't come home.

Sometimes I want to just ask Pleasure, *what the fuck are you doing*

that I'm not doing? Why do my man keep coming back to you? But

that would be crazy as hell. Asking Pleasure that would make her think I'm surrendering or something and I'm not out of the game, yet.

Even though in my heart, I know he is with Pleasure, I can't help but wonder if anything happened to him, car accident or jail. I get up and start pacing the floor for what seemed like hours and just went I'm about to call the hospital to make sure he hasn't been in an accident, I hear his key turn in the door. I make my way back to bed and pretend I am asleep.

FOR MORE INFORMATION ABOUT UPCOMING

RELEASES OR TO CONTACT PATTI DOSS

EMAIL: pattiedoss@gmail.com

WEBSITE: www.authoresspattidoss.com

www.exquisitereadspublications.com

FACEBOOK: AUTHORESS PATTI DOSS

TWITTER: @Authoress_Patti

www.ingramcontent.com/pod-product-compliance
Lightning Source LLC
Chambersburg PA
CBHW030353020726
47493CB00003B/804